studio collections

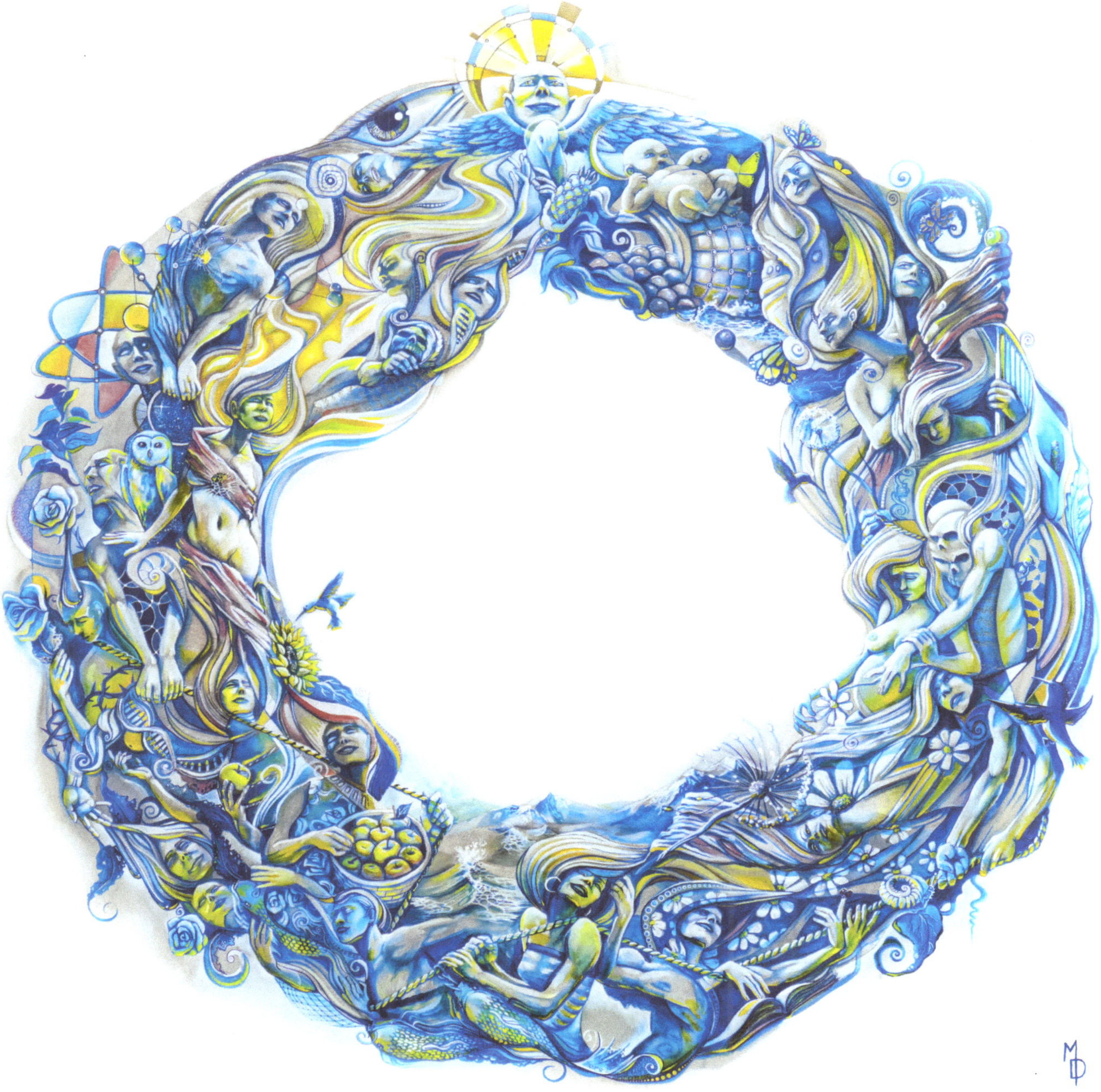

Art by Miles Davis | The Totem Series

Studio Collections | Art by Miles Davis - The Totem Series

Massive Burn Studios
www.massiveburn.com

First Edition 2024

ISBN 979-8-9918816-0-9

Artwork by Miles Davis
Cover Design and Typeset by Merissa Corbet Davis

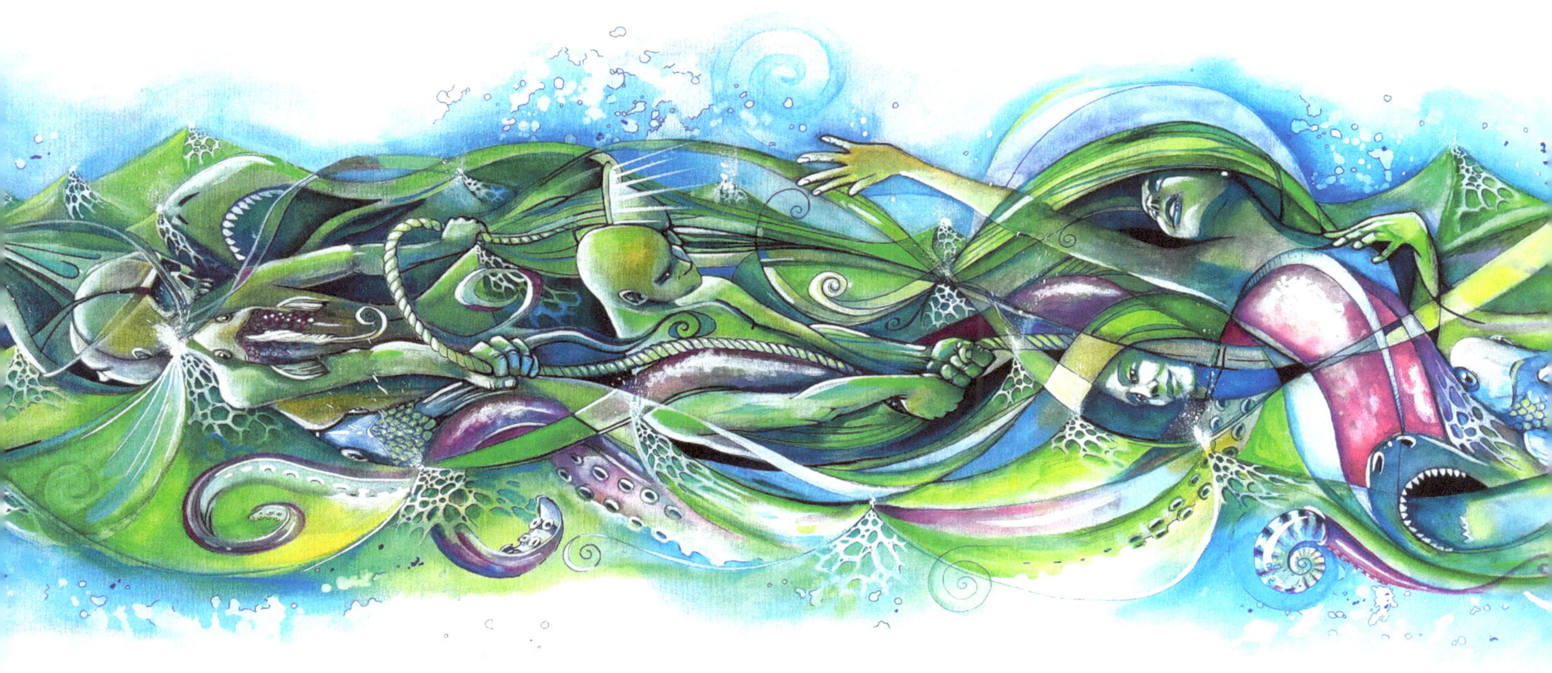

The Totem Series

Discover the Totem Series by Miles Davis – a series of neosurrealistic paintings exploring the actions and reactions of one's life. Signified by curves and movement that unearth figures, these paintings tell stories of the internal spirit.

Metamorphosis, 2019
24"x48"
Acrylic & Mixed Media on Canvas

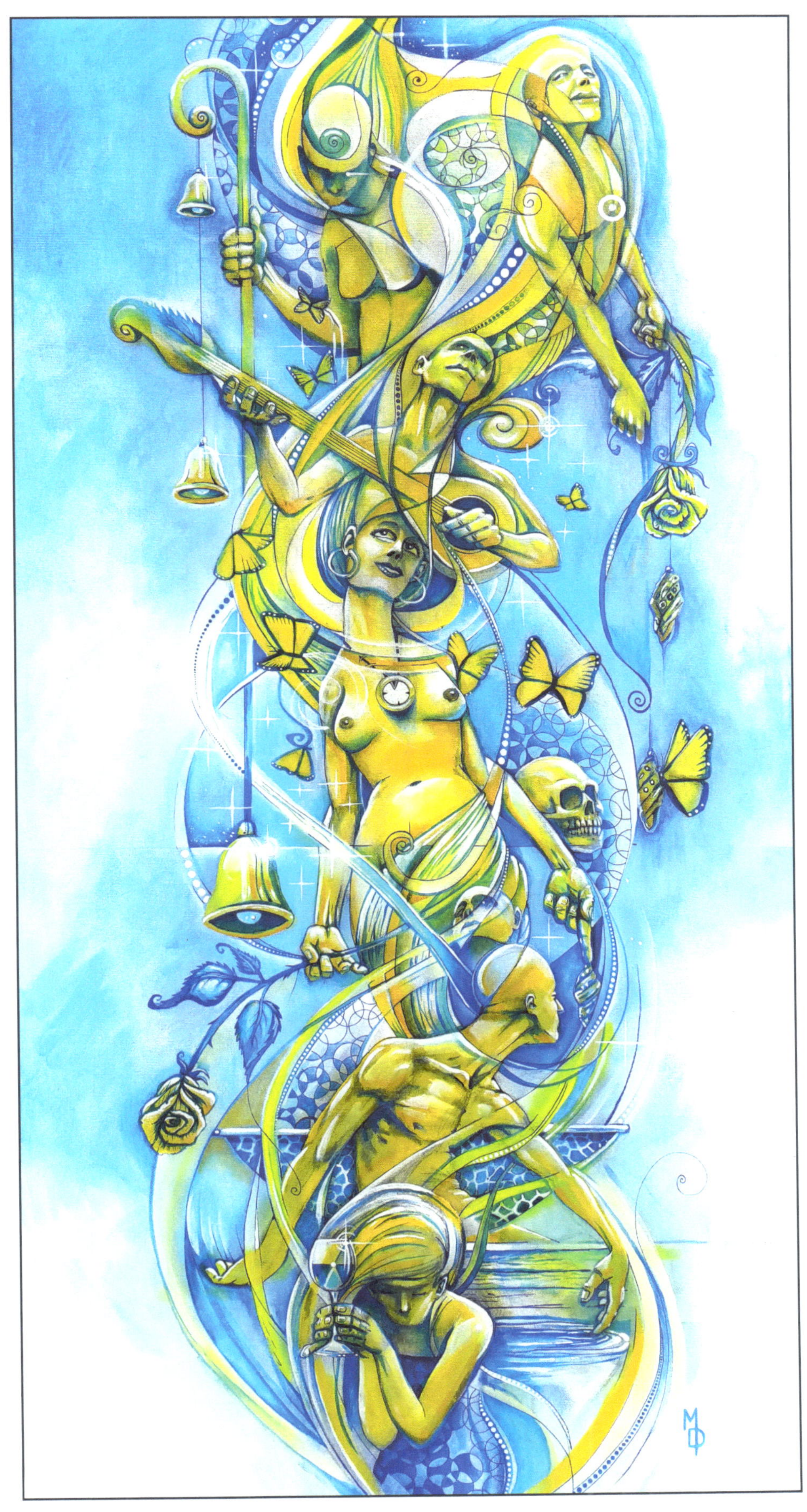

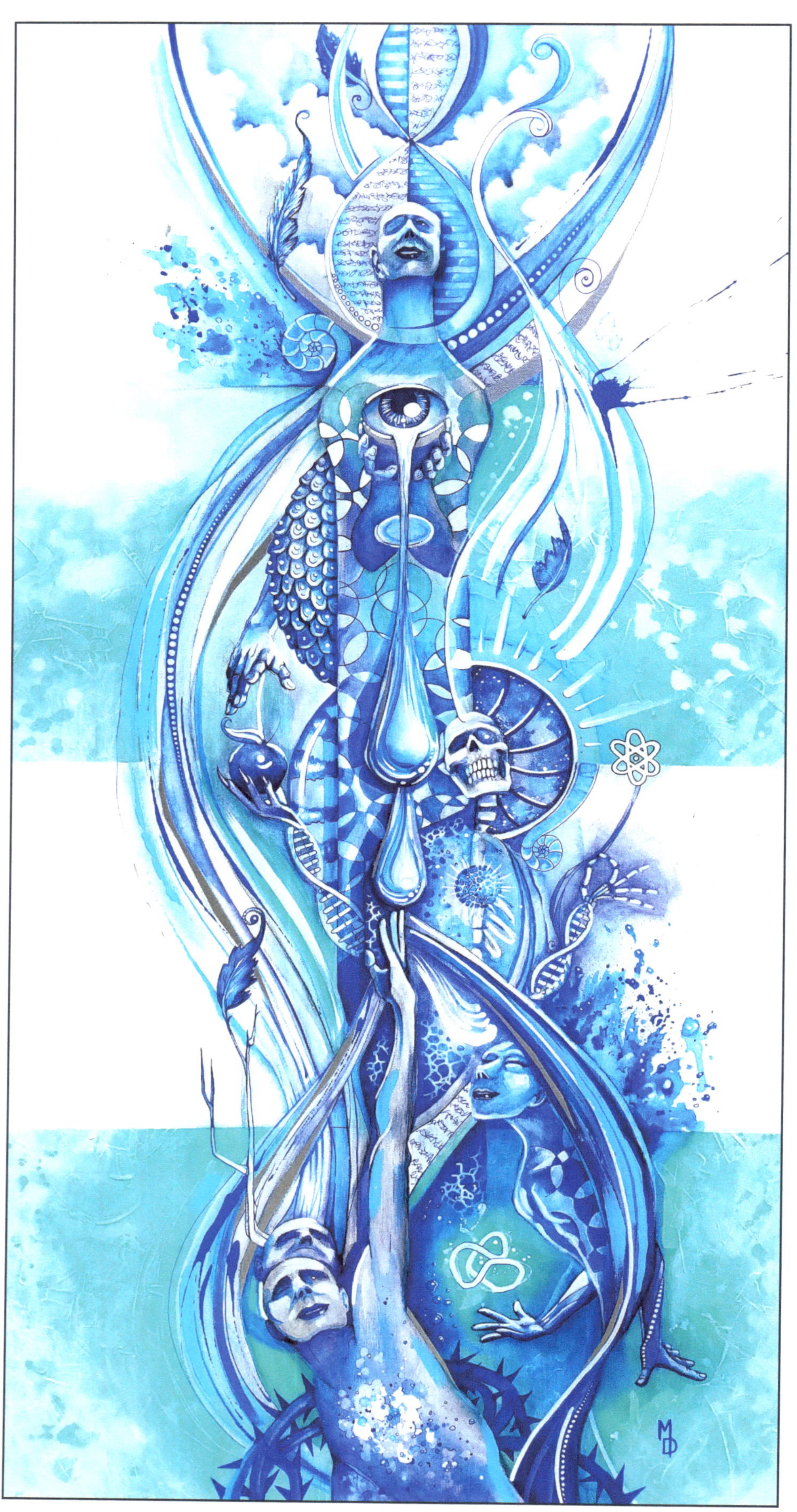

Osmosis, 2019
24"x48"
Acrylic & Mixed Media on Canvas

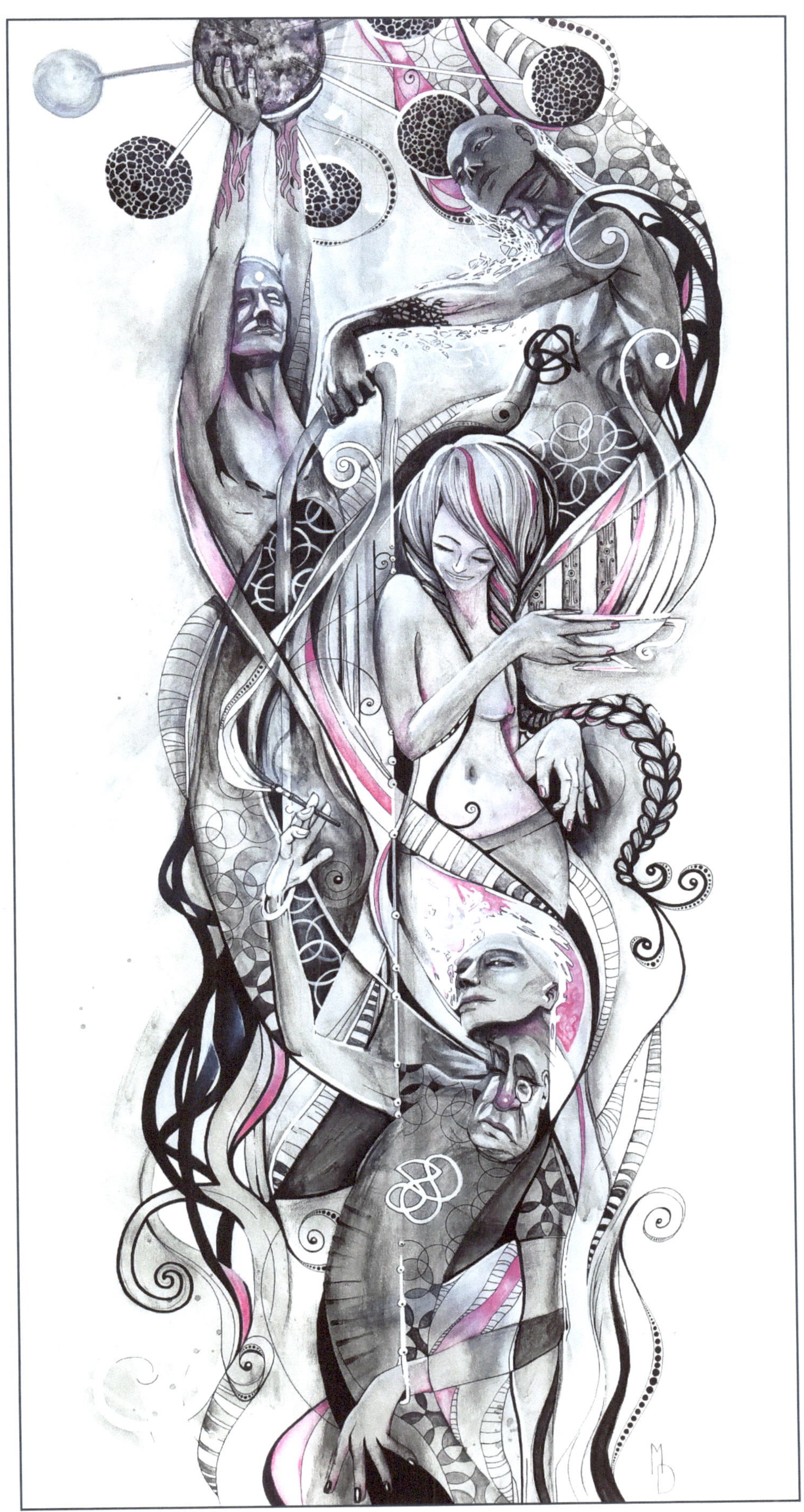

Infusion, 2019
24"x48"
Acrylic & Mixed Media on Canvas
In the Permanent Collection of the Marietta Cobb Museum of Art

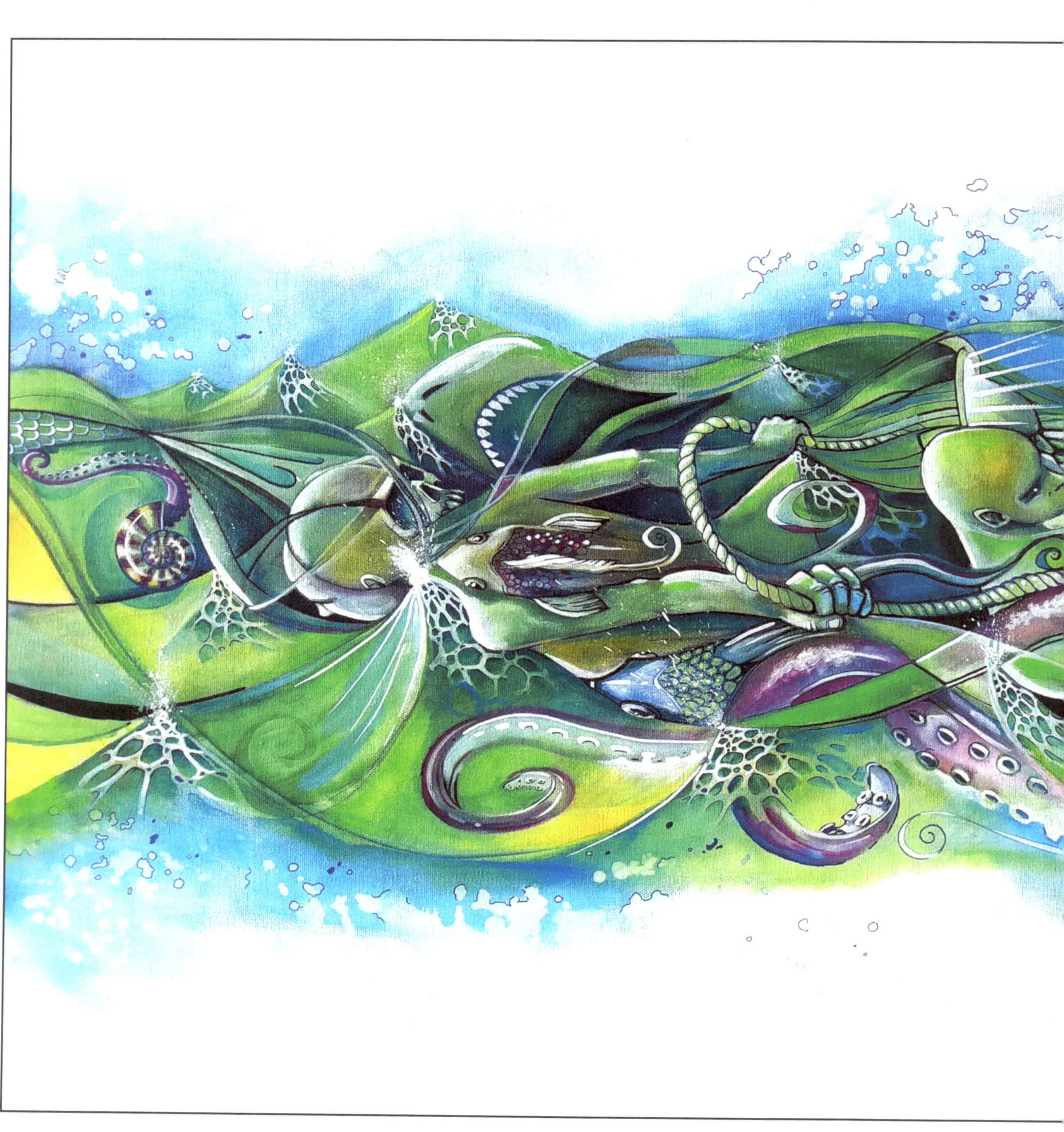

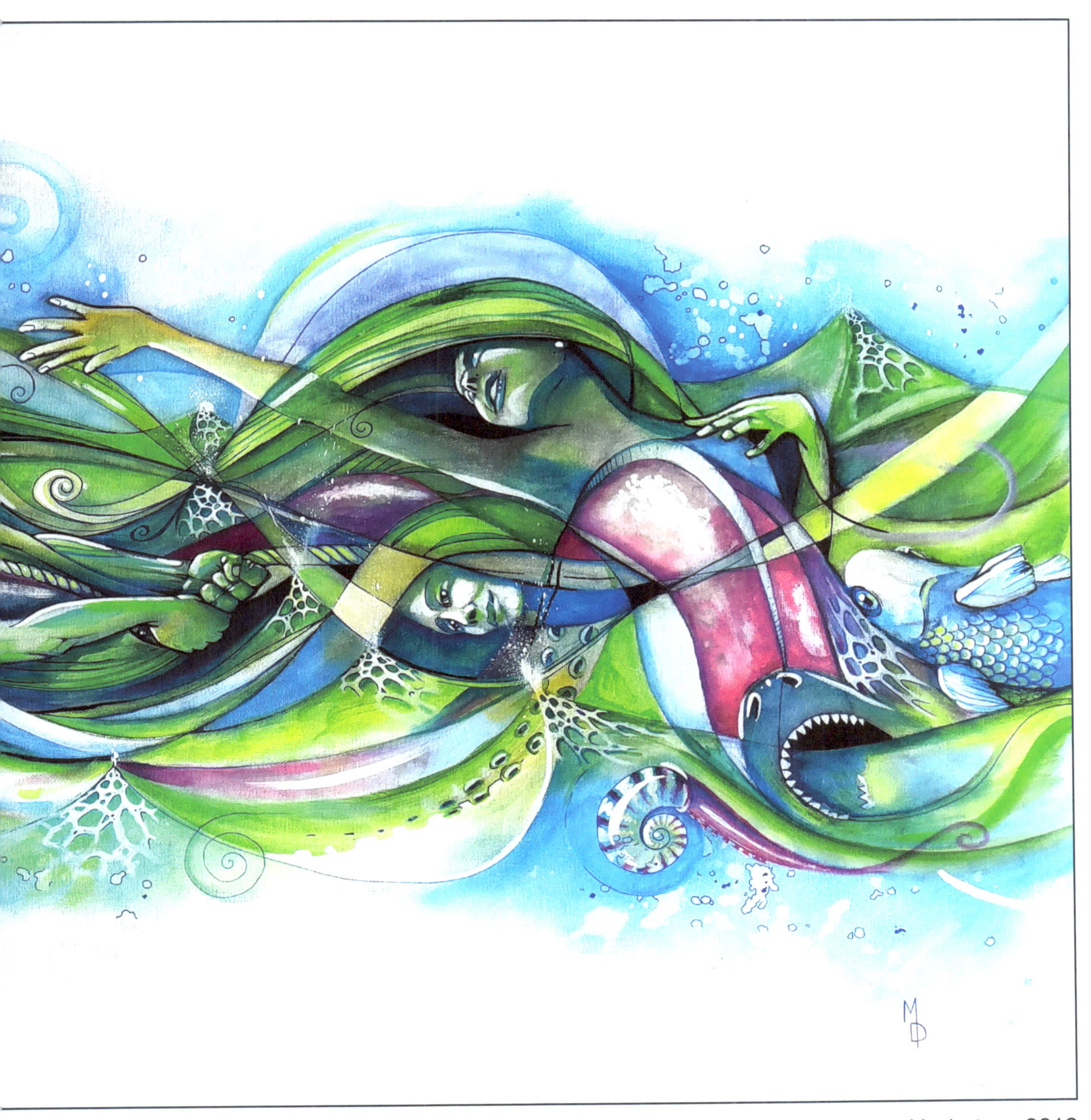

Undertow, 2019
48"x24"
Acrylic & Mixed Media on Canvas

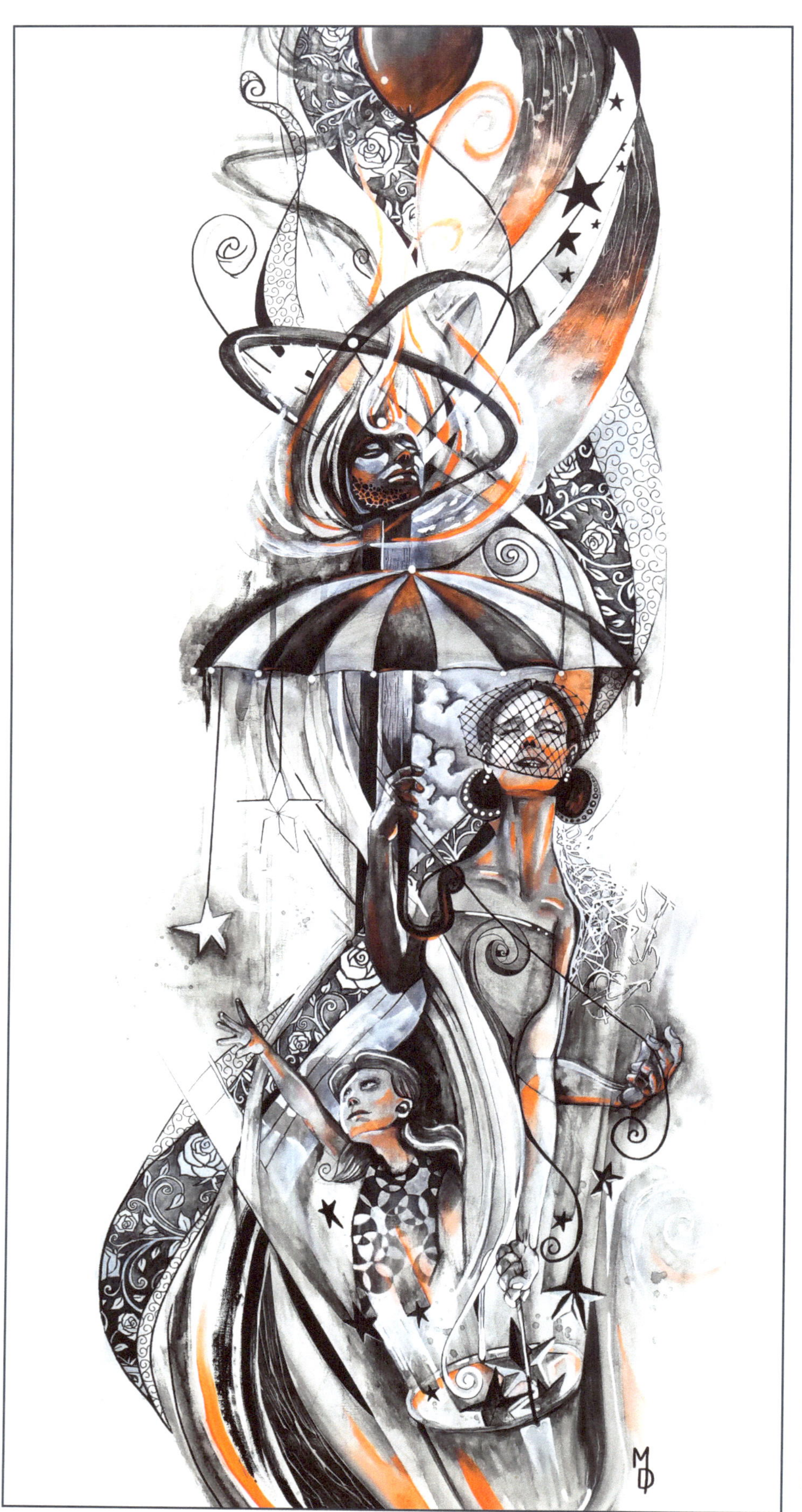

Fire & Rain, 2019
24"x48"
Acrylic & Mixed Media on Canvas
Blacklight Enhanced

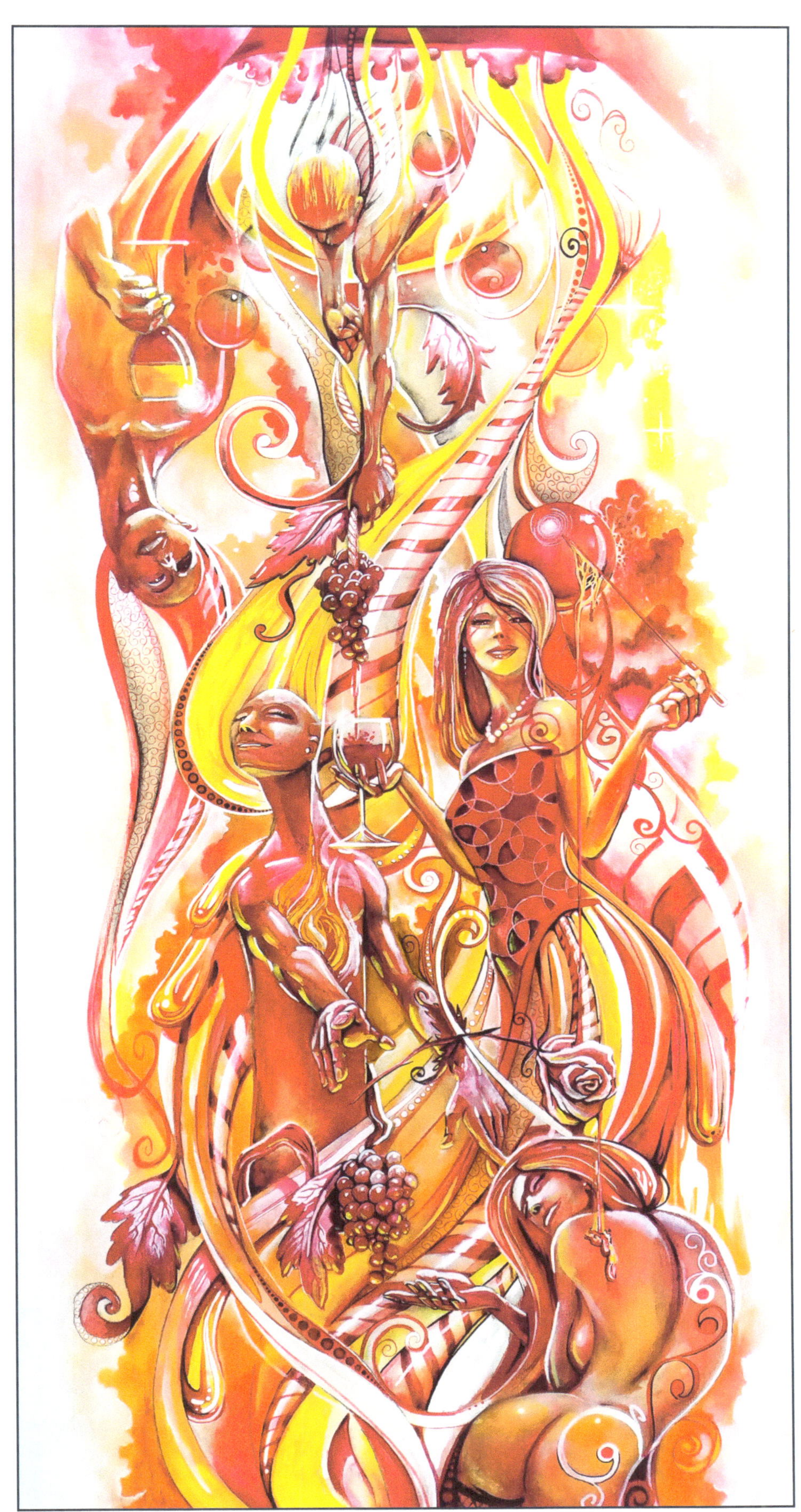

Peppermint Nectar, 2020
24"x48"
Acrylic & Mixed Media on Canvas

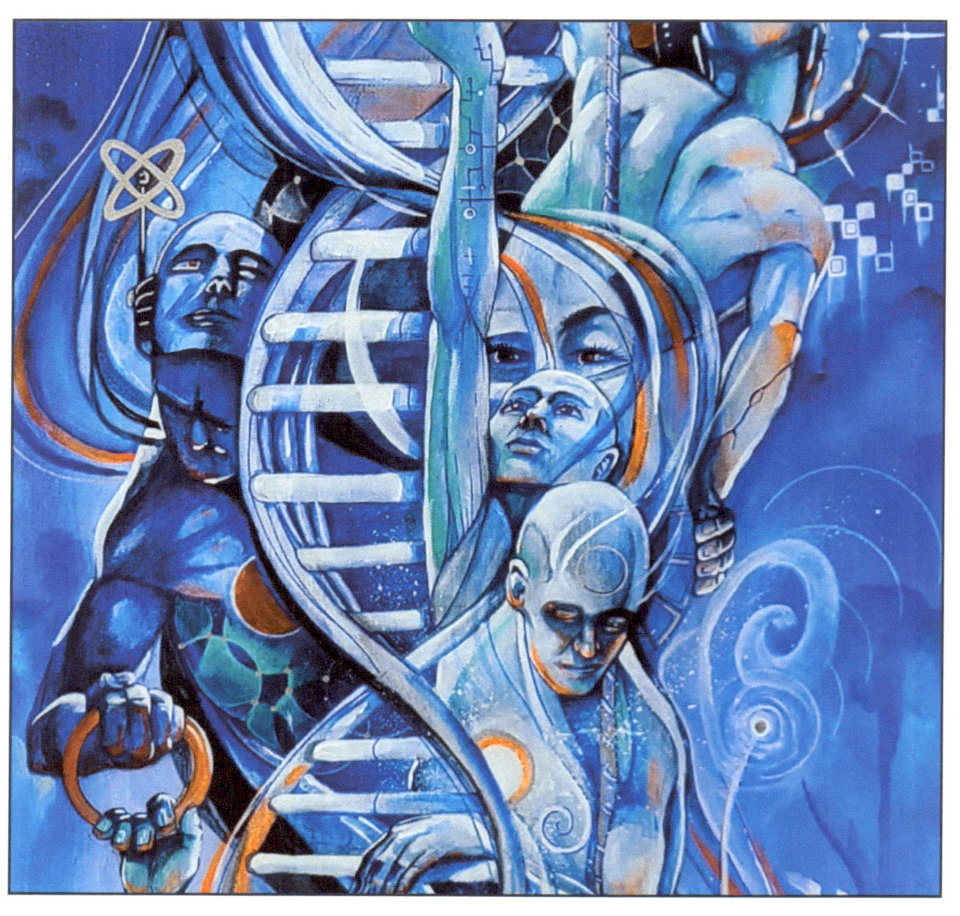

"When I started *Jacob's Ladder,* I had just finished some research into genetic and cyber engineering and my imagination ran wild with thoughts of the human species' evolution into the future."

Jacob's Ladder, 2020
24"x48"
Acrylic & Mixed Media on Canvas
Blacklight Enhanced

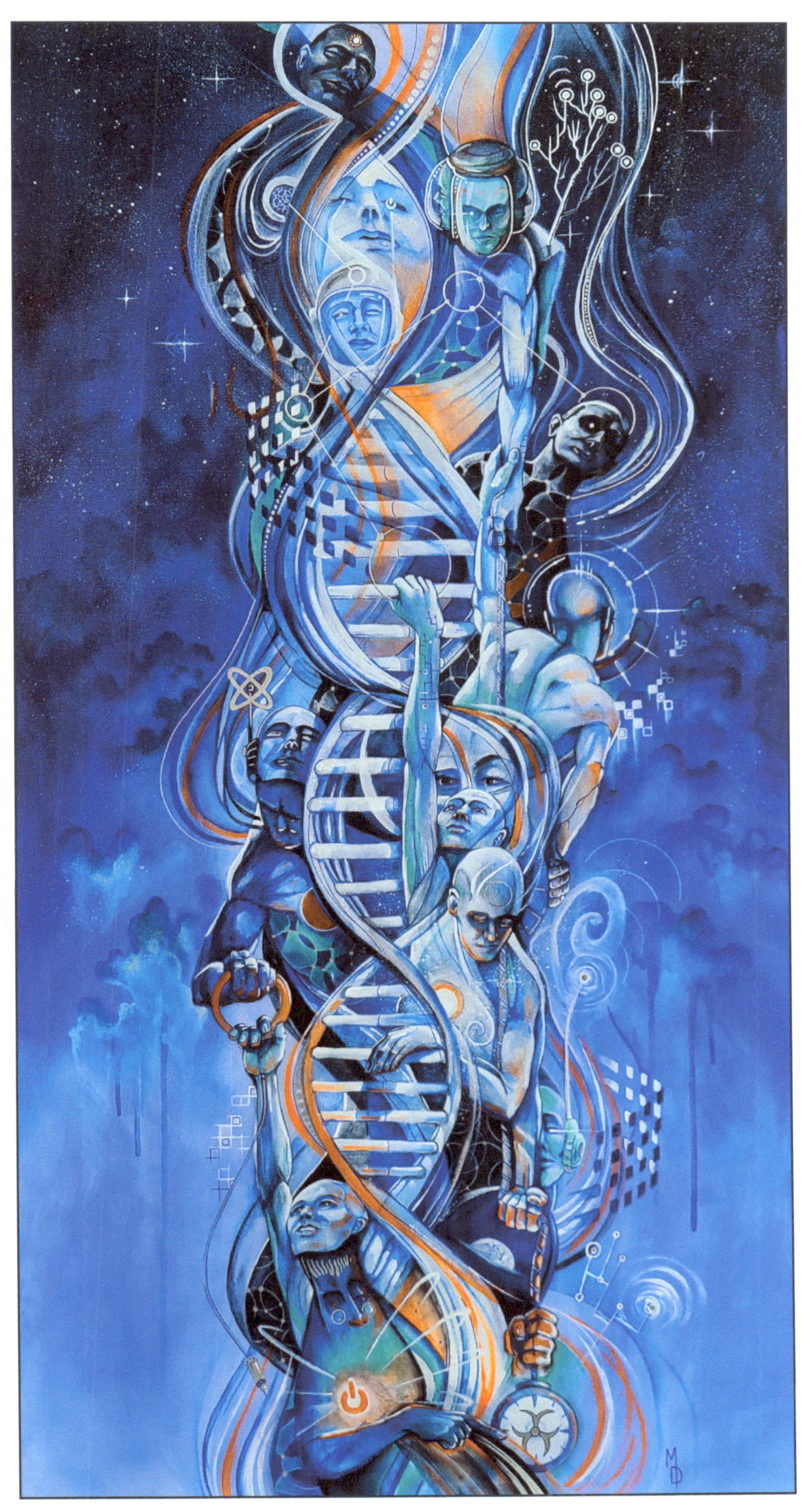

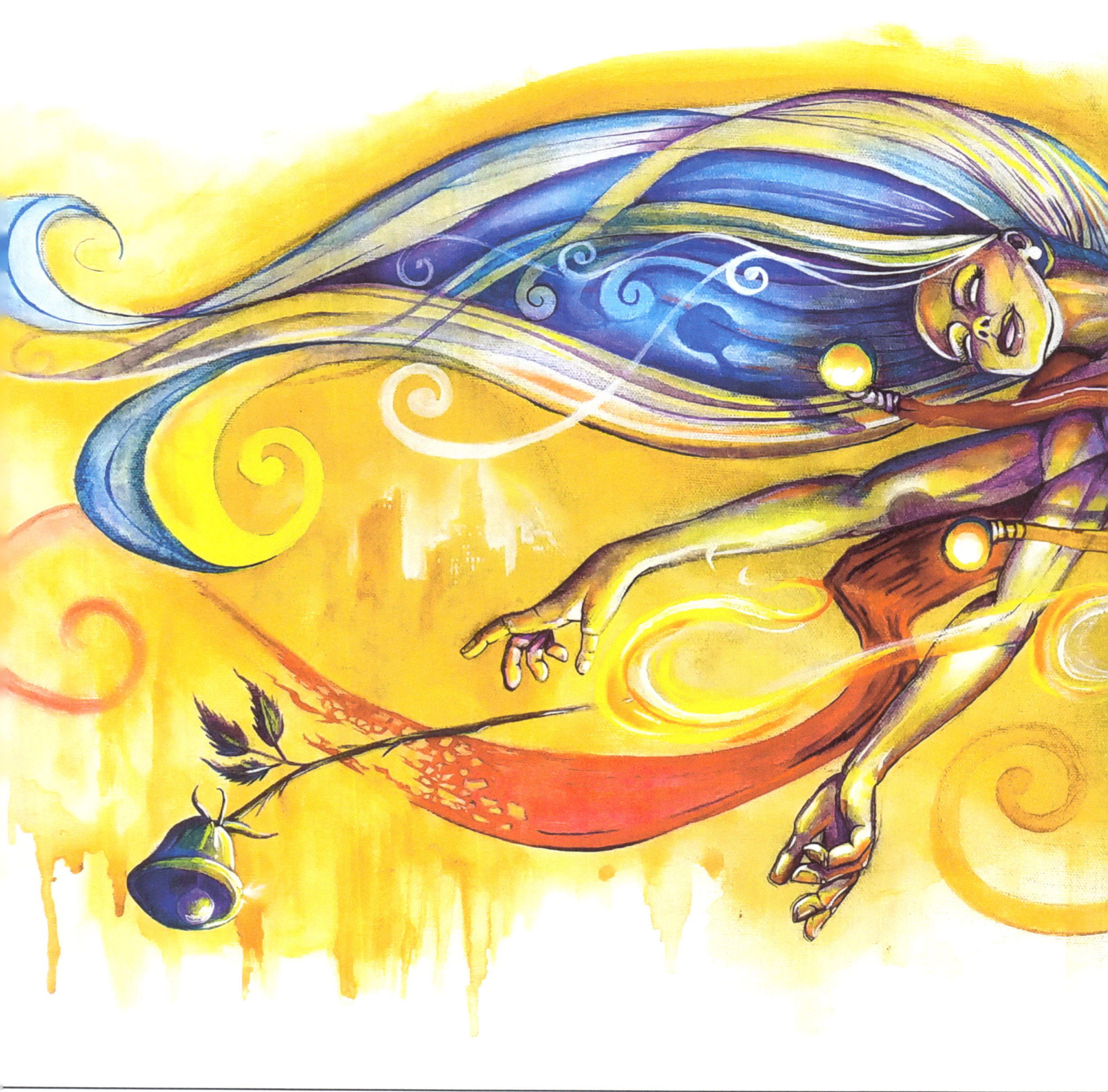

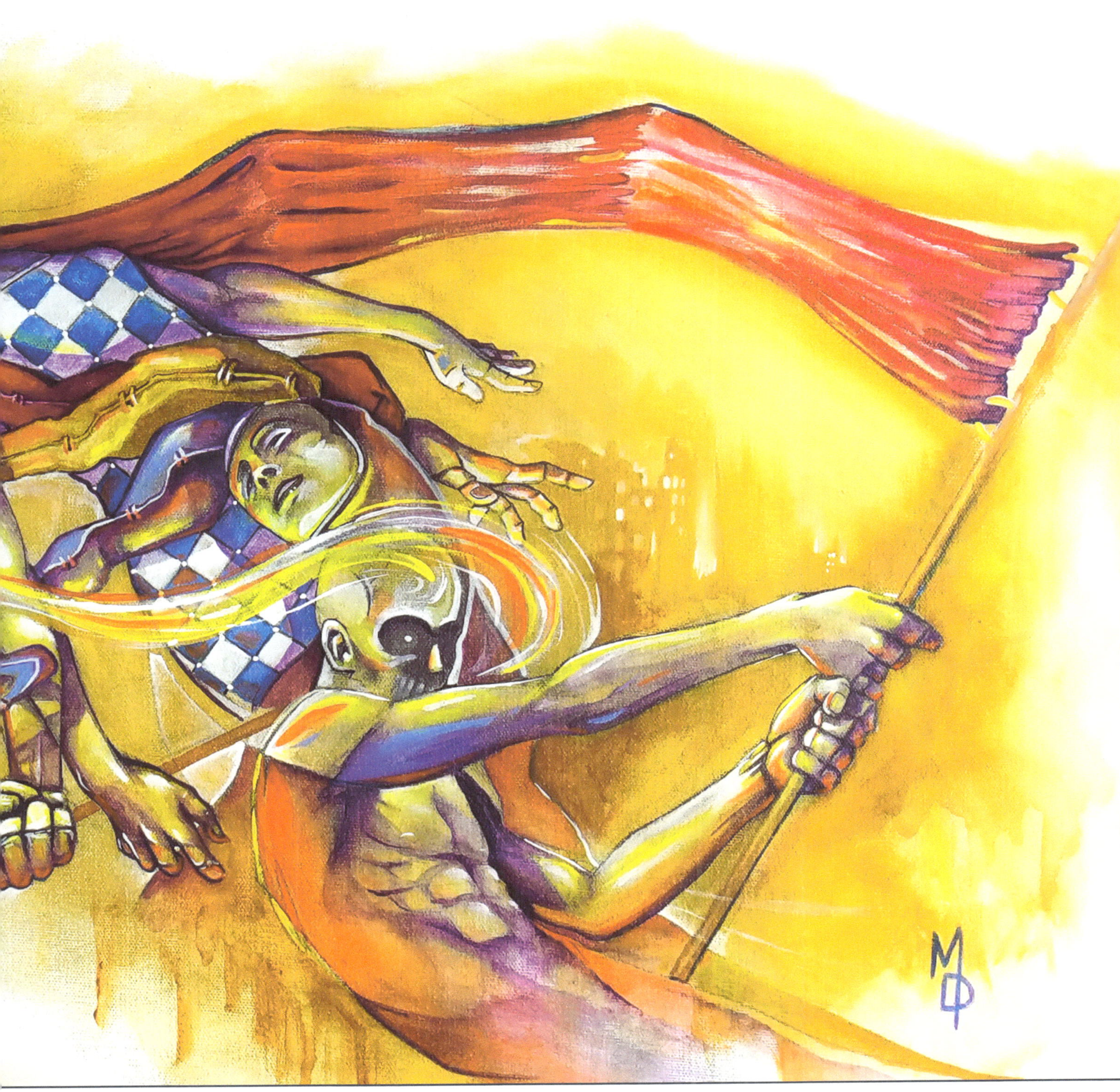

Spirit of Rebellion, 2020
36"x18"
Acrylic & Mixed Media on Canvas

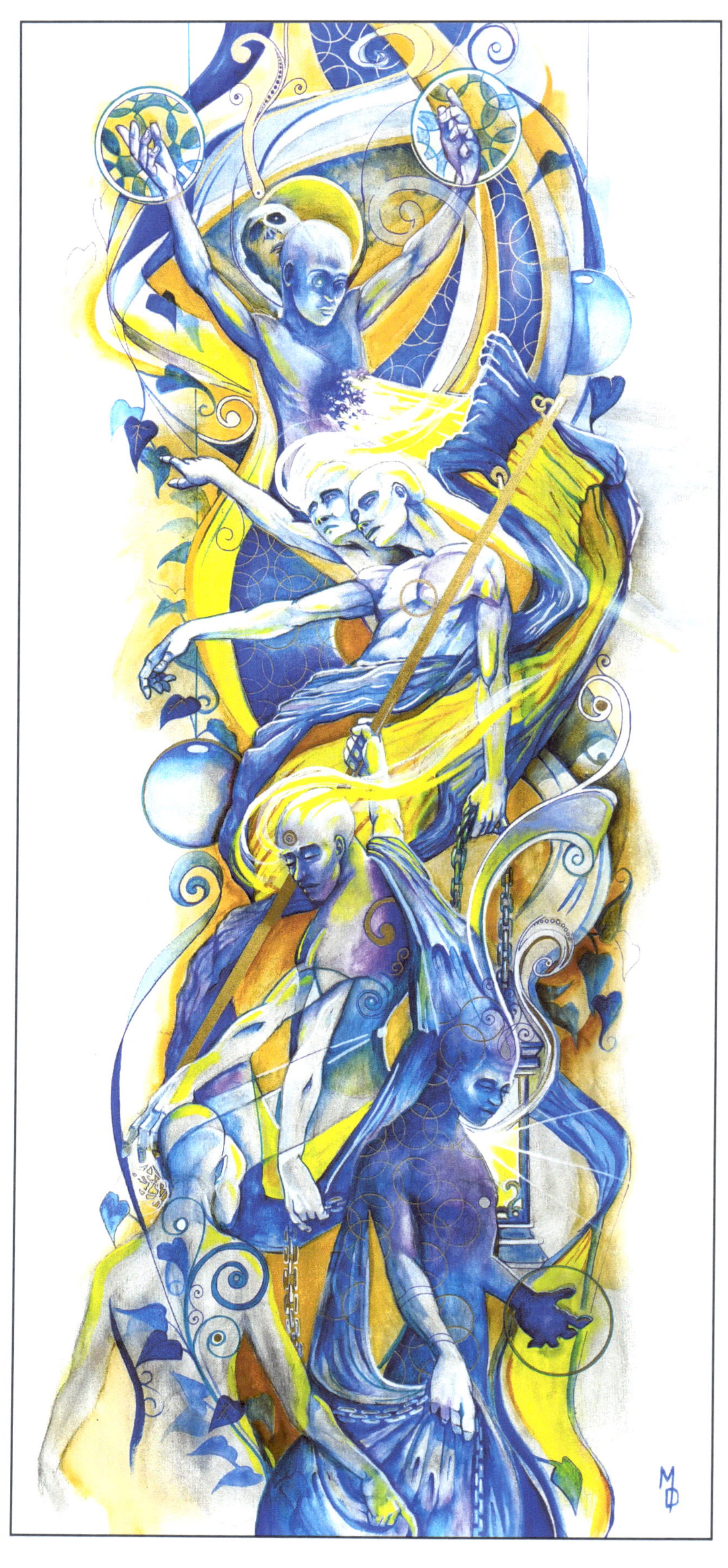

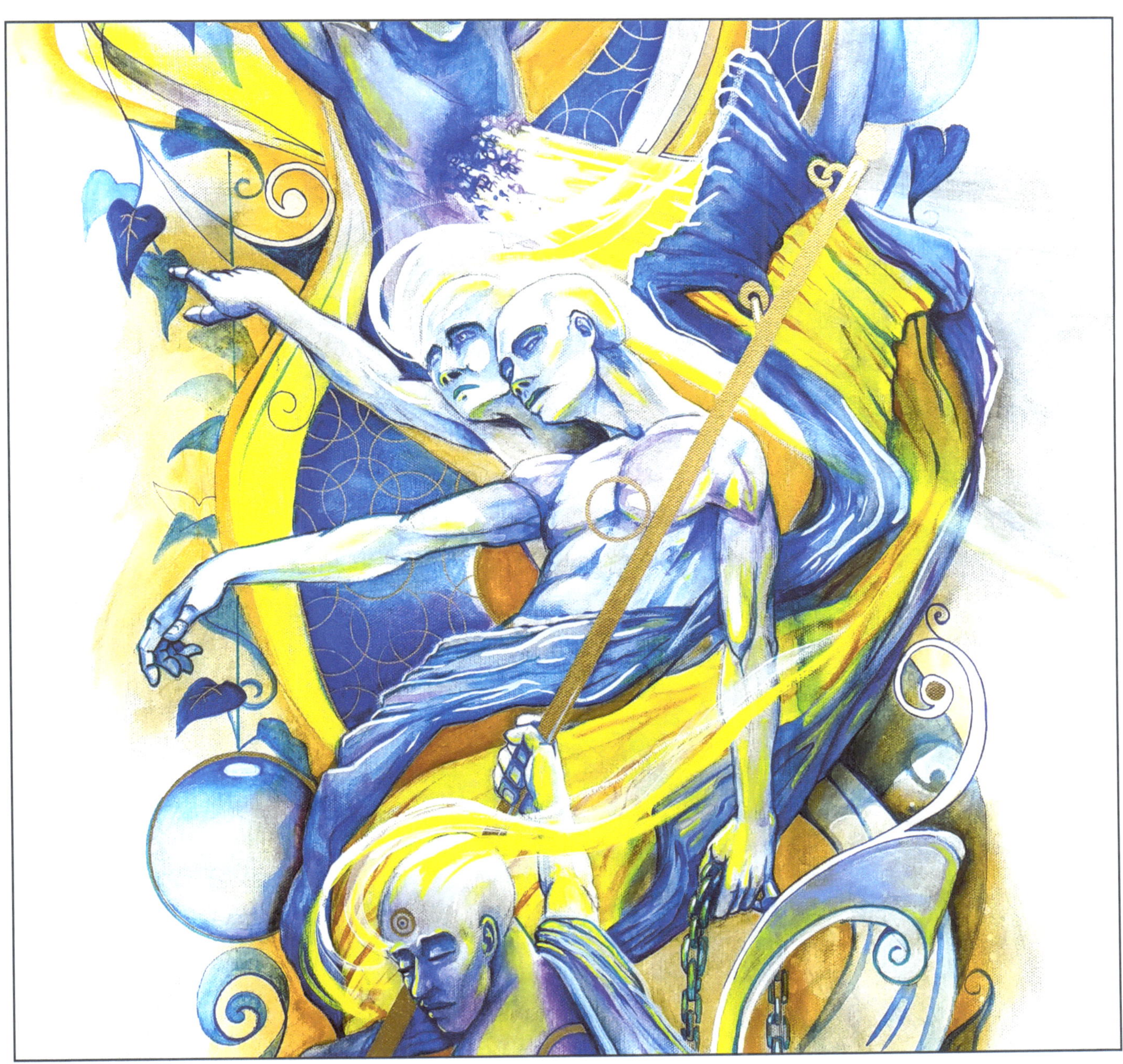

Photosynthesis, 2020
24"x48"
Acrylic & Mixed Media on Canvas

Illuminating the Legacy encapsulates the spark of inspiration as a candle flame churning with the toils of believing in one's self.

***Illuminating the Legacy*, 2021**
24"x48"
Acrylic & Mixed Media on Canvas

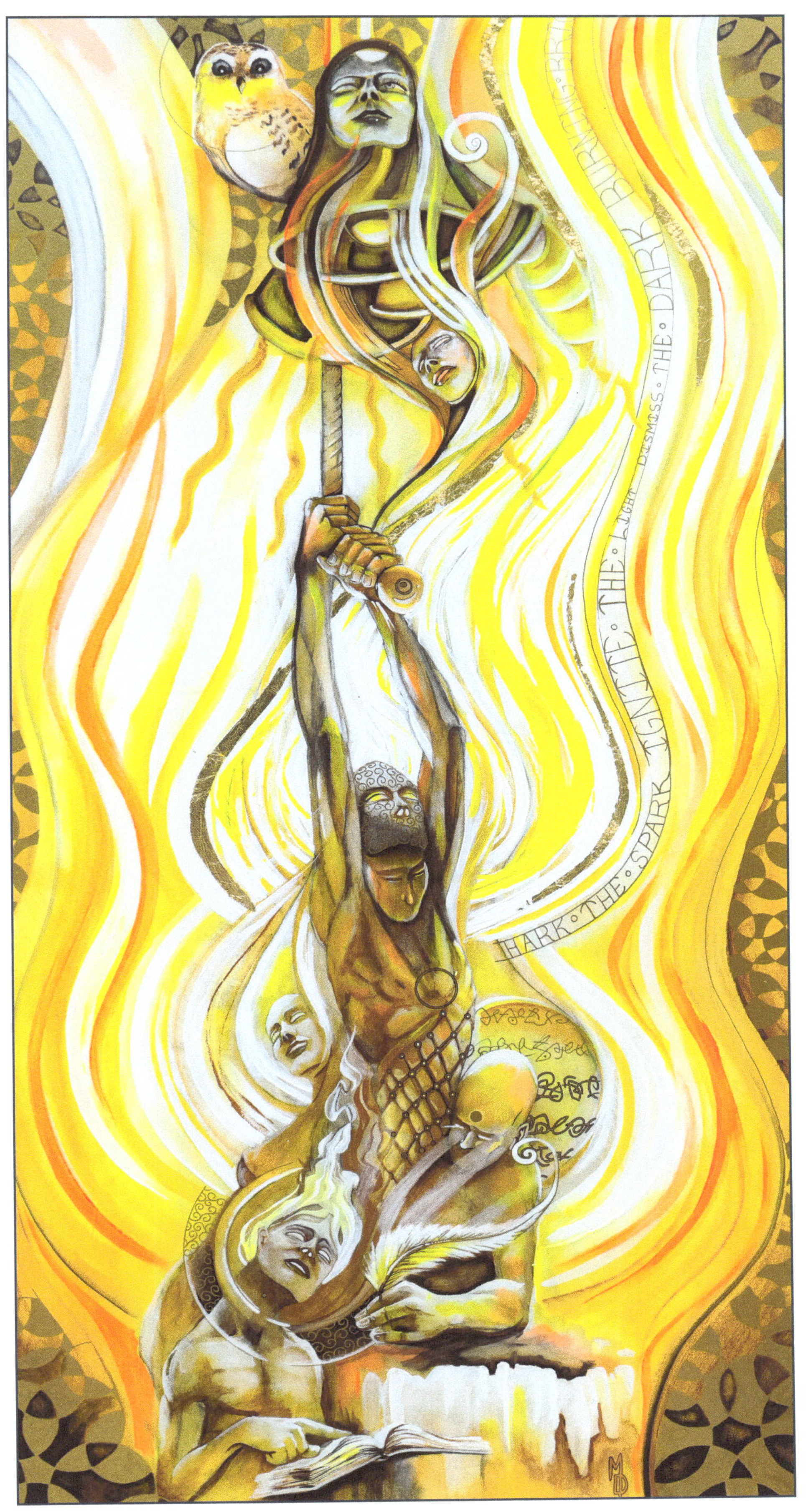
HARK · THE · SPARK · IGNITE · THE · LIGHT · DISMISS · THE · DARK · BURNING

"I incorporate my learning into my final work, for better or worse. I rarely use models or reference materials in my work, typically preferring to create from imagination after my research."

Learning Curve, 2020
30"x40"
Acrylic & Mixed Media on Canvas

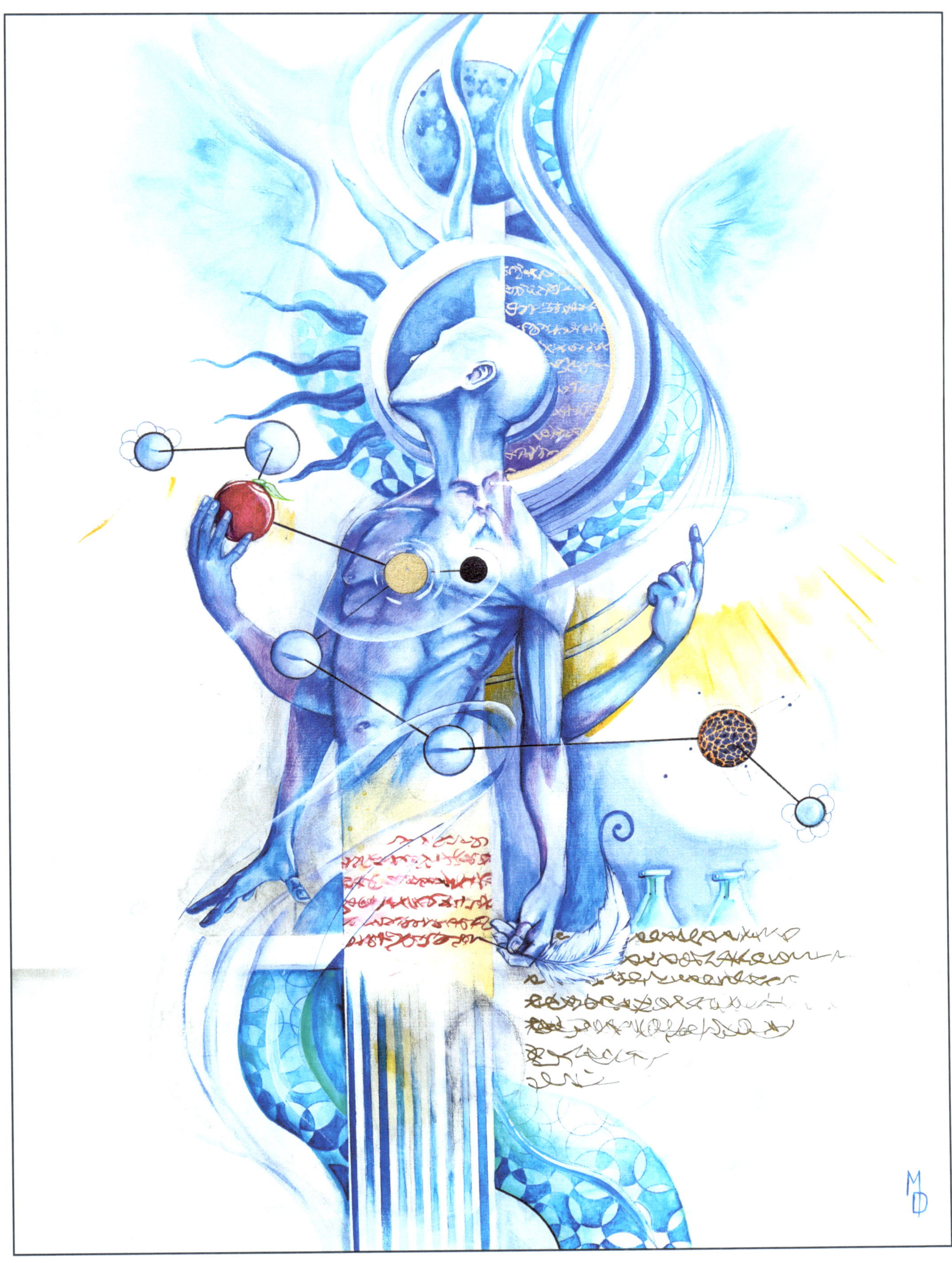

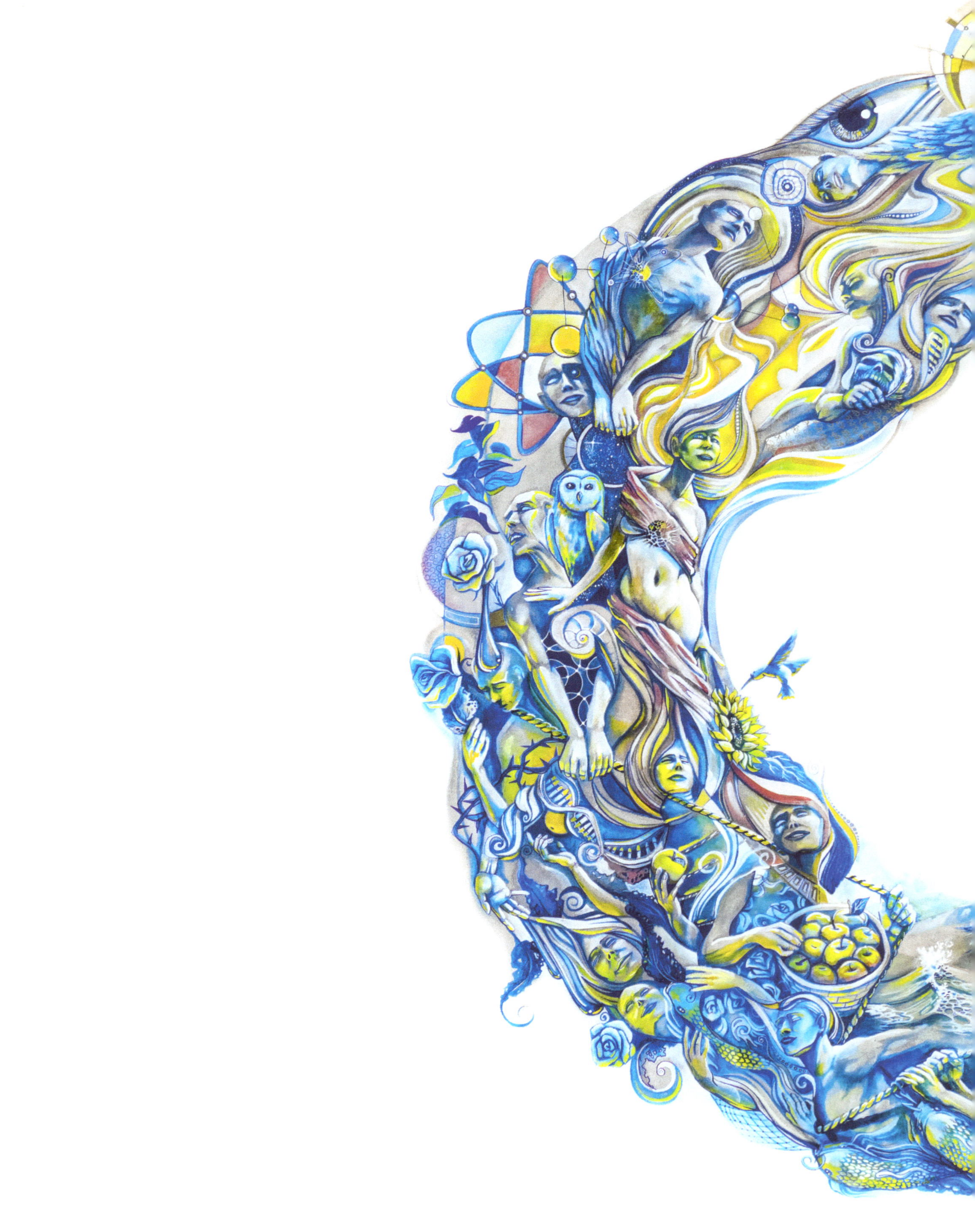

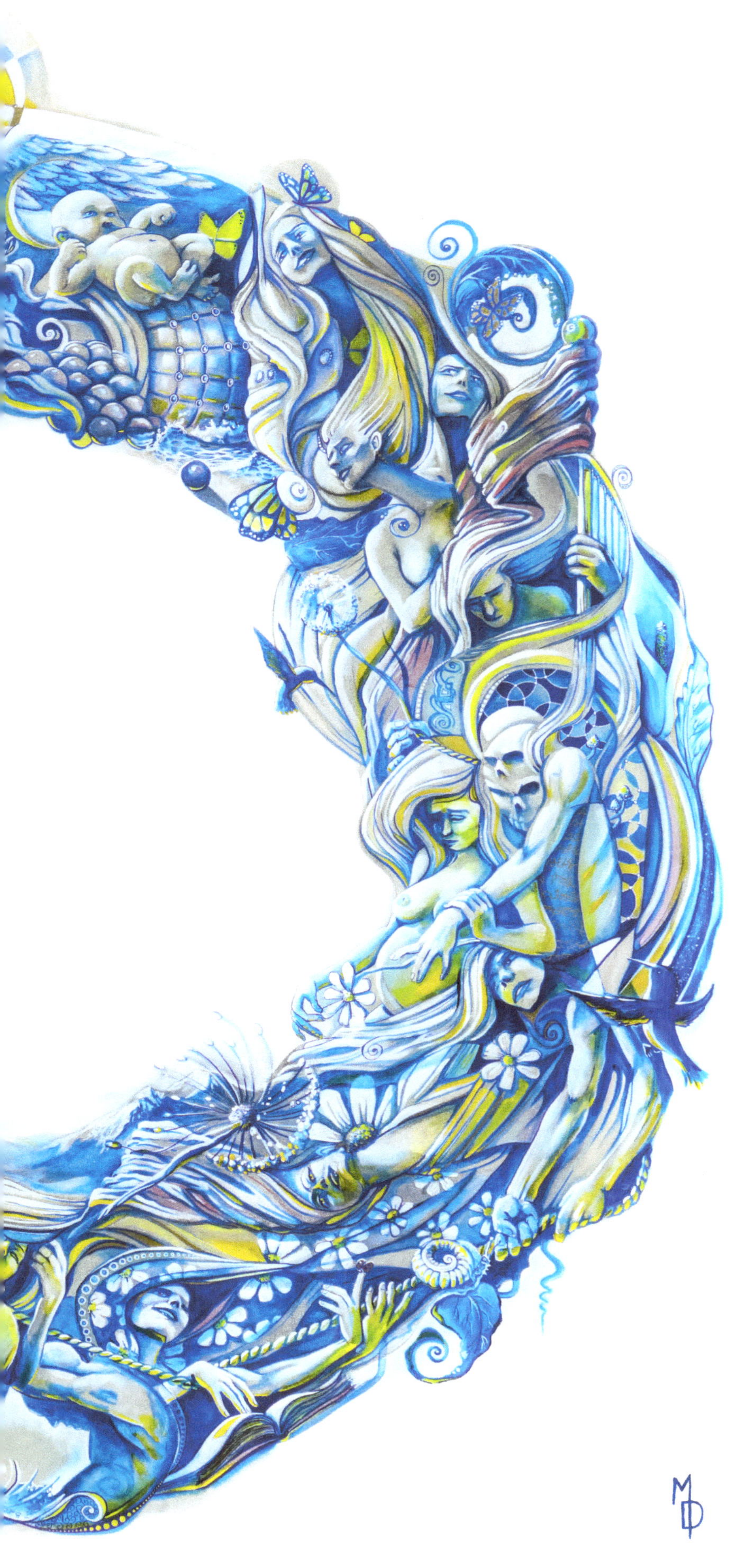

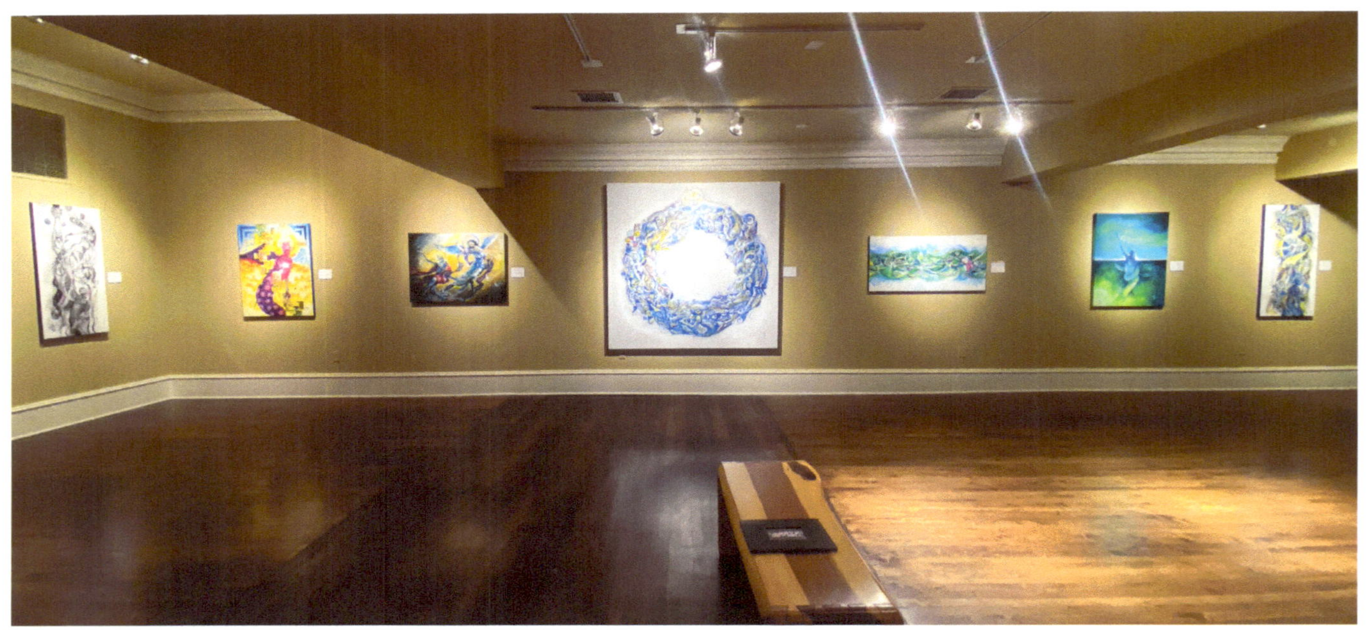

Vibrant Shadows Solo Exhibition, Marietta Cobb Museum of Art, Marietta, GA, USA. Photo courtesy of Magnus Fleming.

"The circle carries so many symbolic meanings to me, like cycles or infinity, so it was a great compositional choice for *Seasons of Wither* discussing the existential life cycle of a woman."

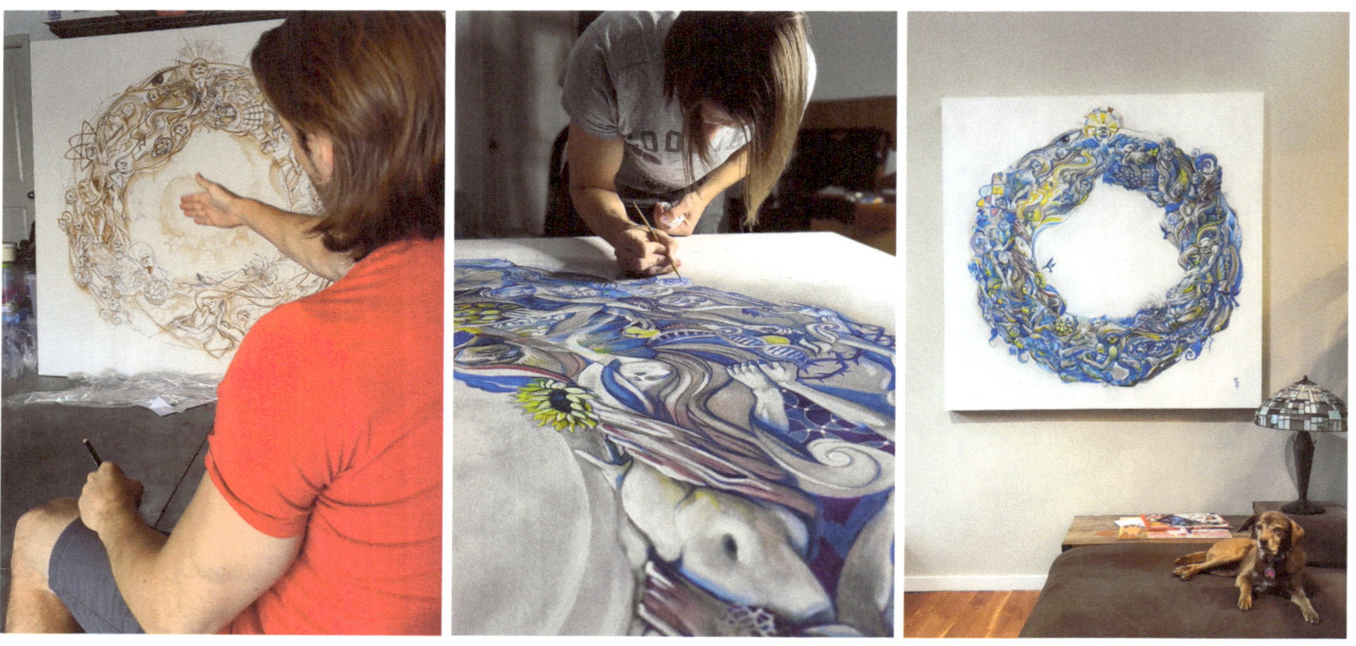

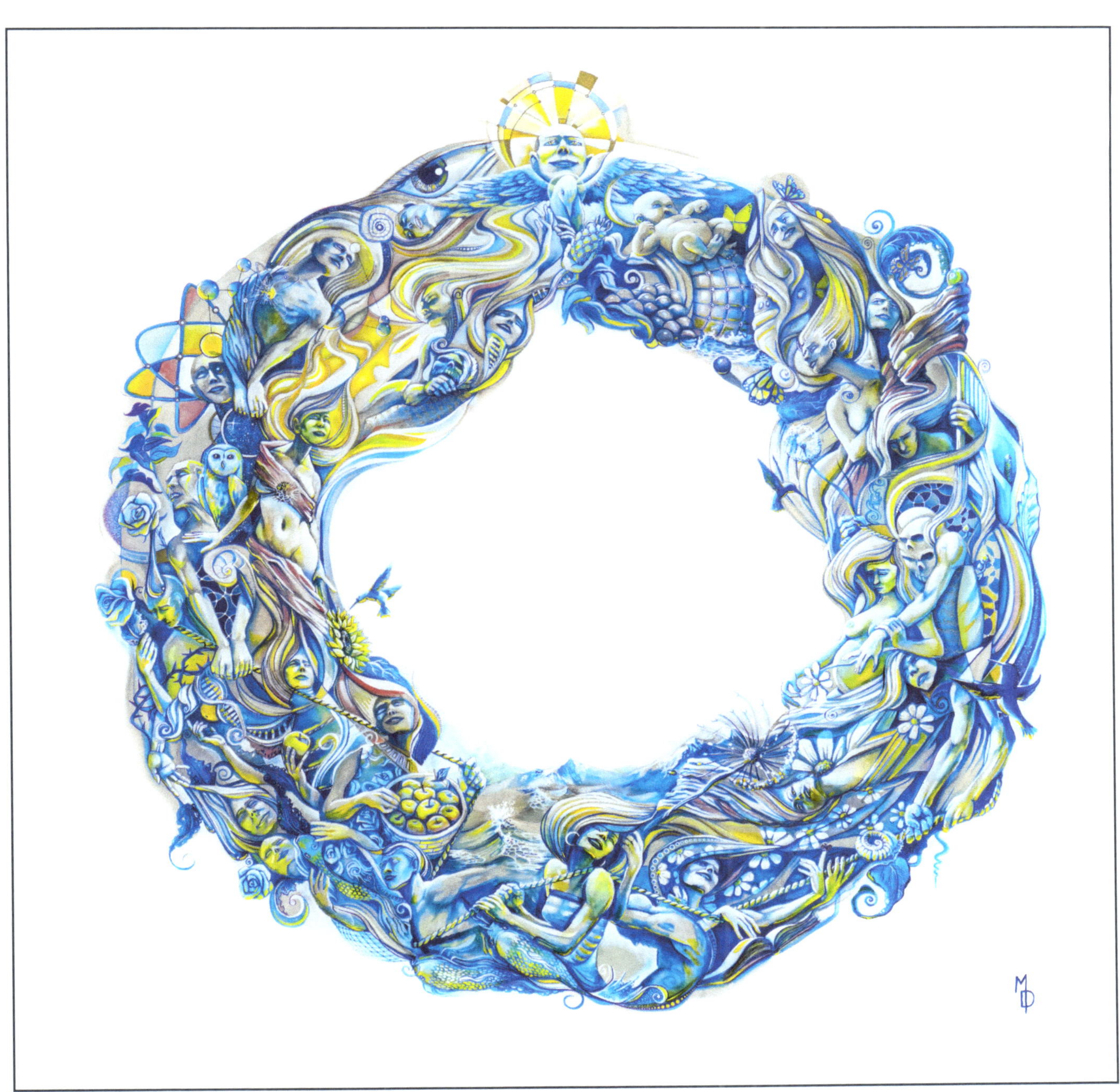

Seasons of Wither, 2022
72"x72"
Acrylic & Mixed Media on Canvas

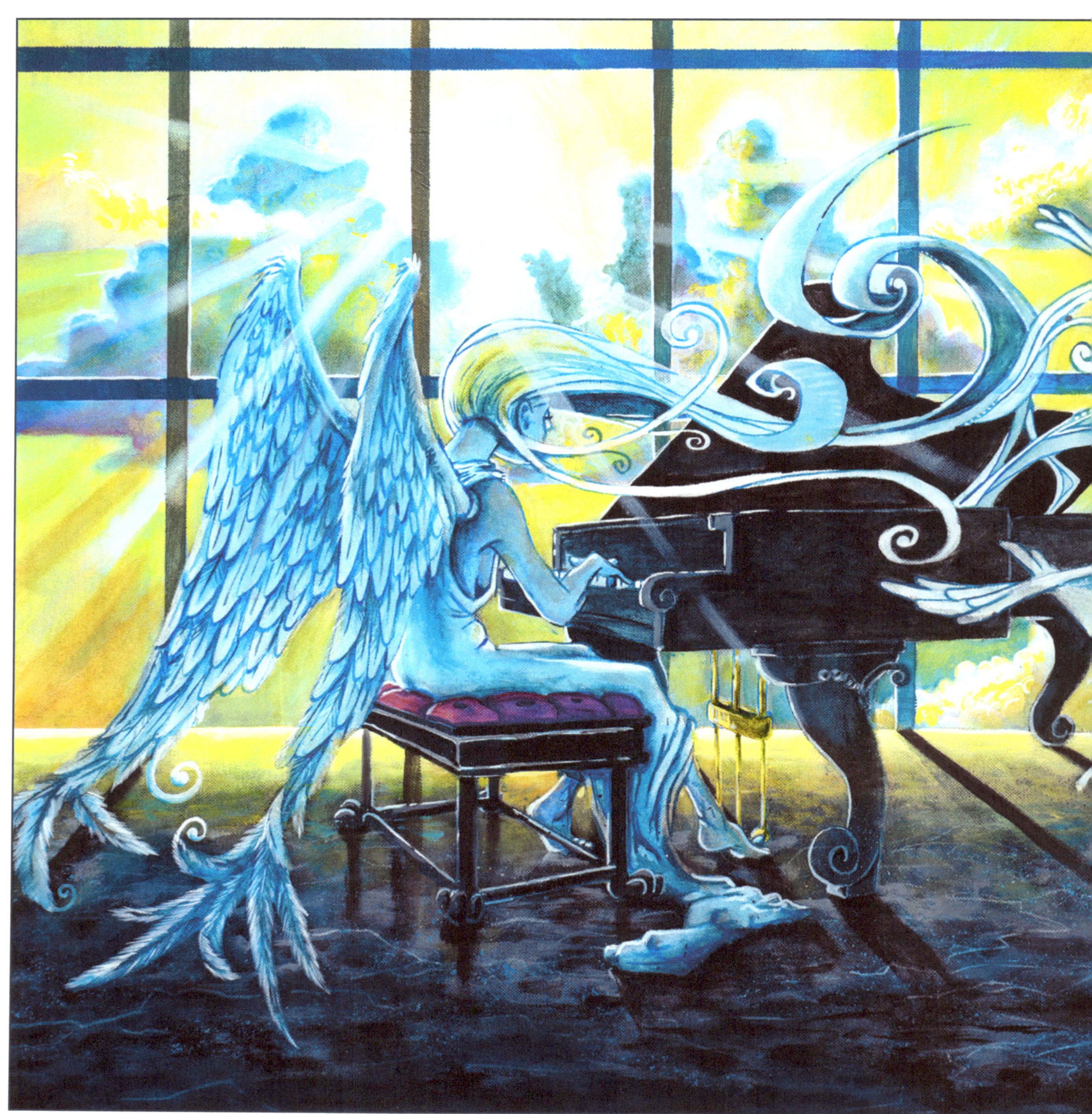

Beginnings

Prior to the Totem Series, Miles had explored the utilization of flowing lines as compositional elements in a few earlier works, with *Pandora's Keys* representing the first example of this style.

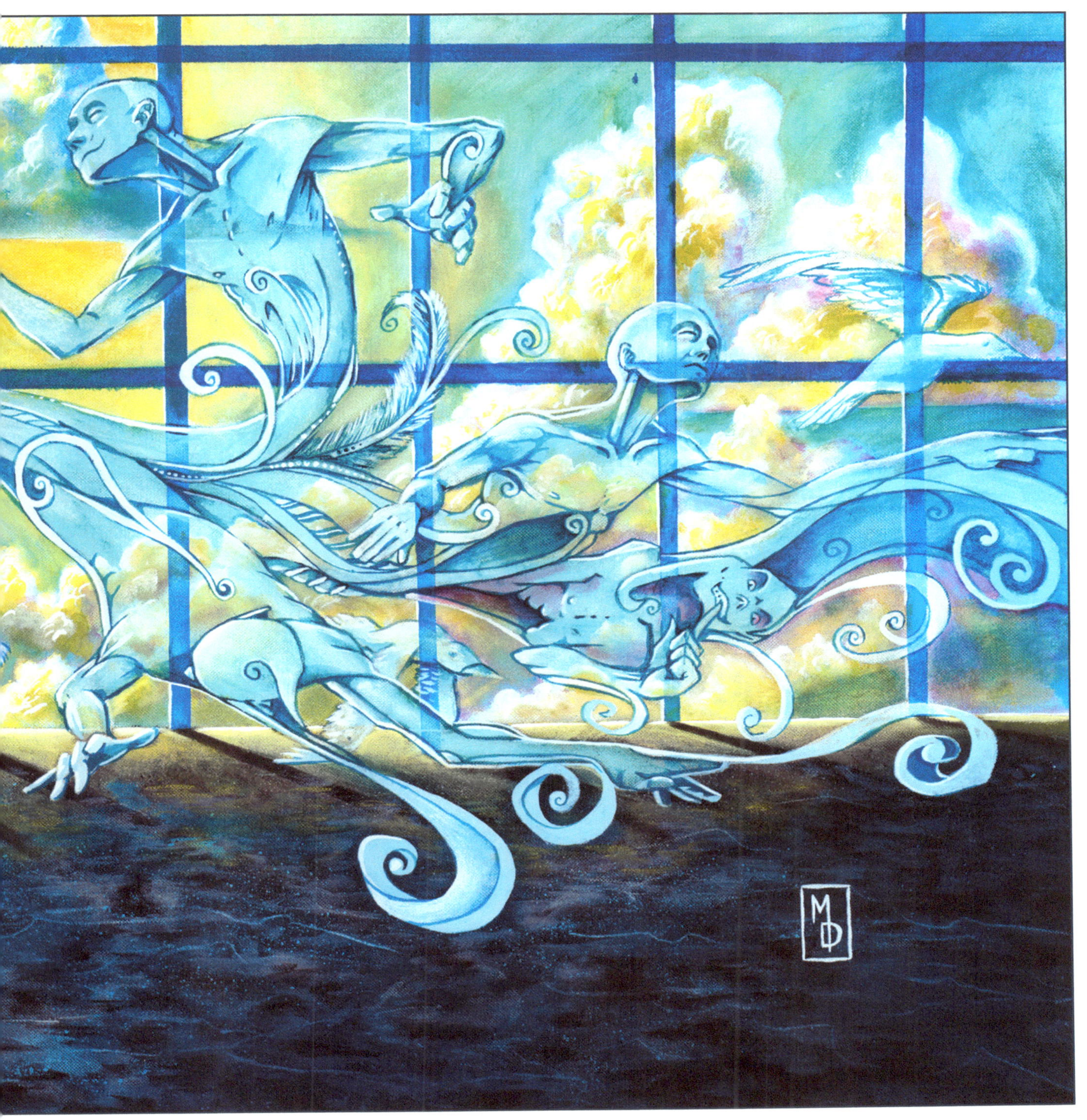

Pandora's Keys, 2010
48"x24"
Acrylic & Mixed Media on Canvas

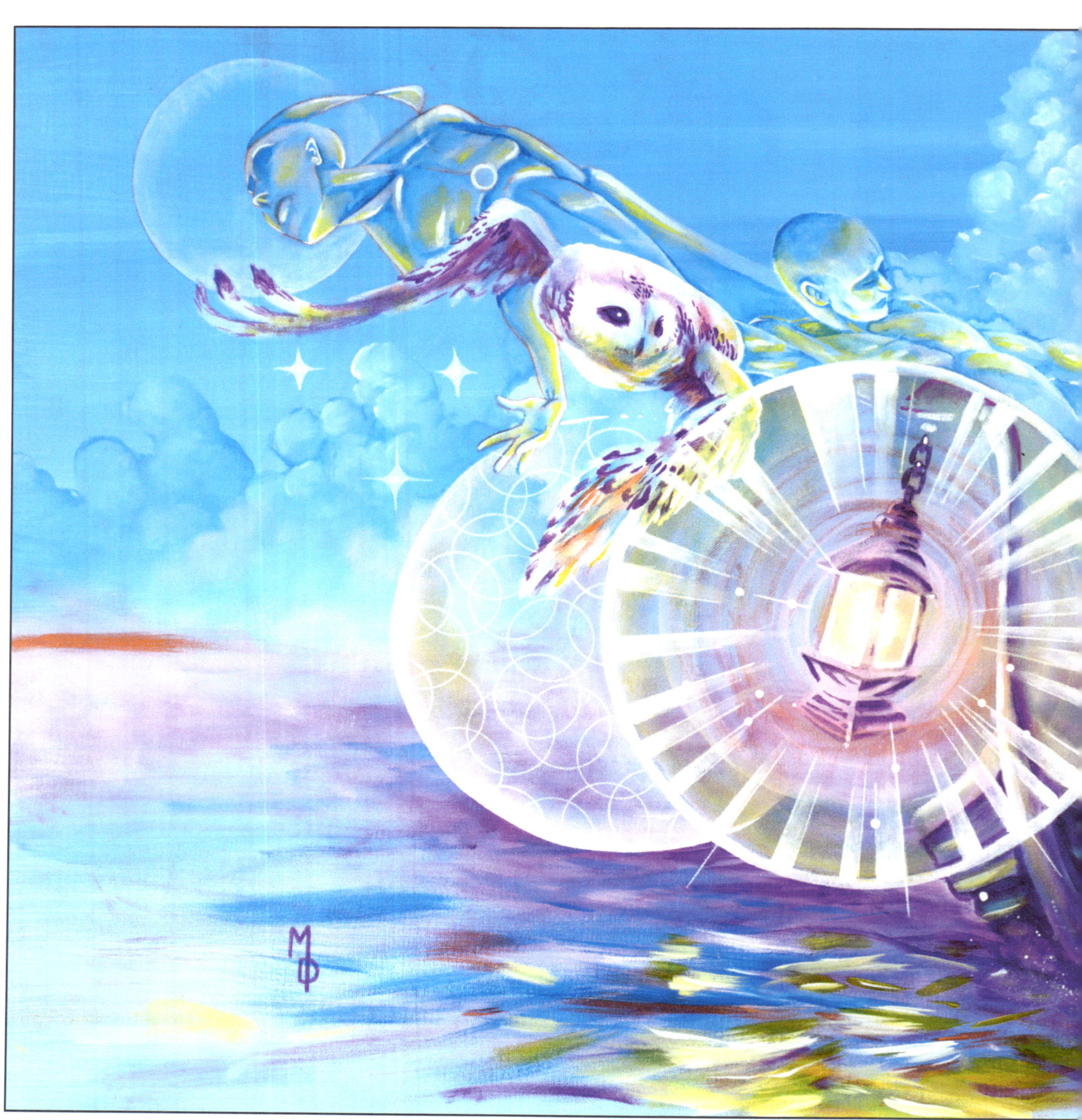

Minion of Styx, 2014
48"x24"
Acrylic & Mixed Media on Canvas

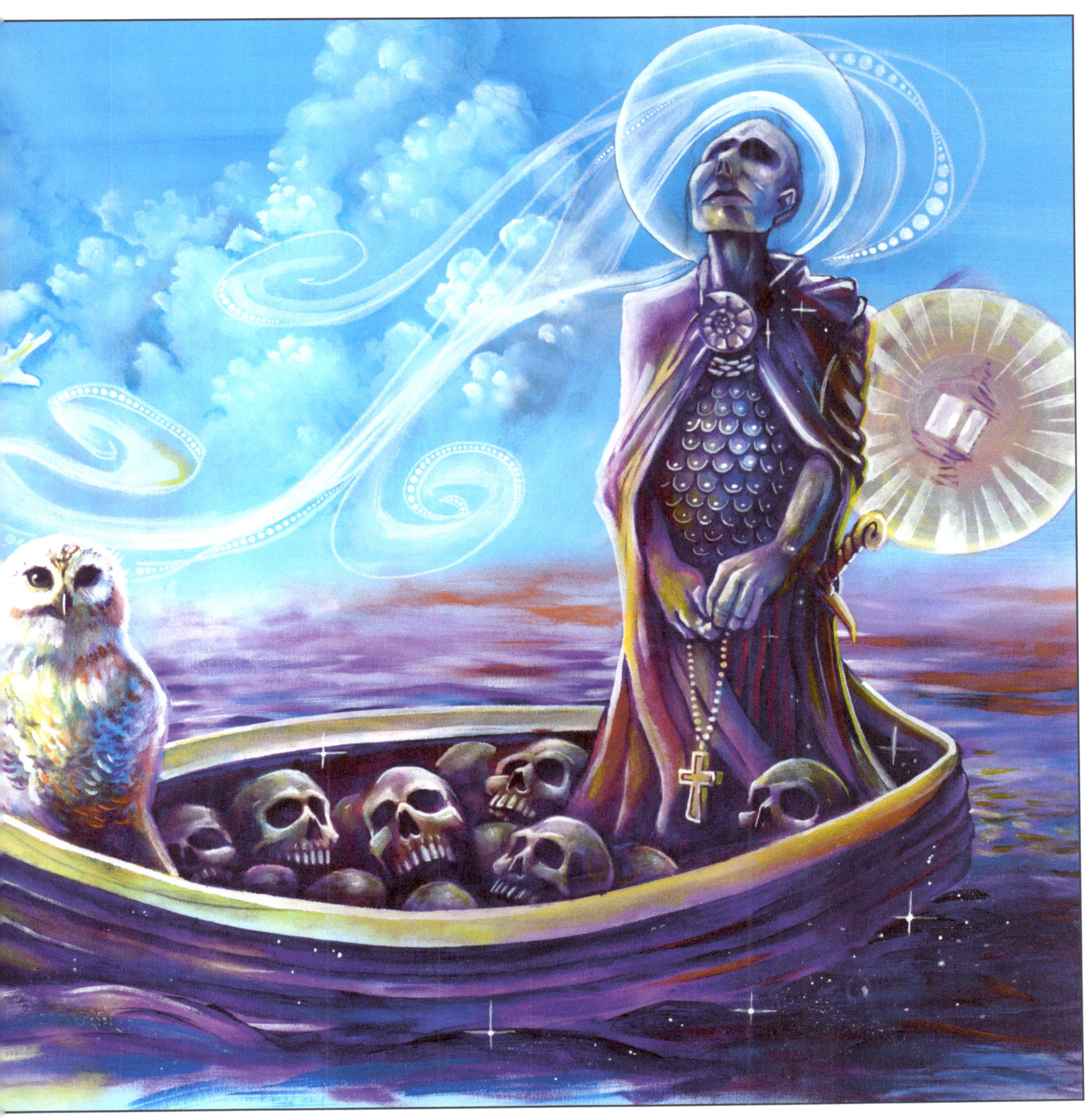

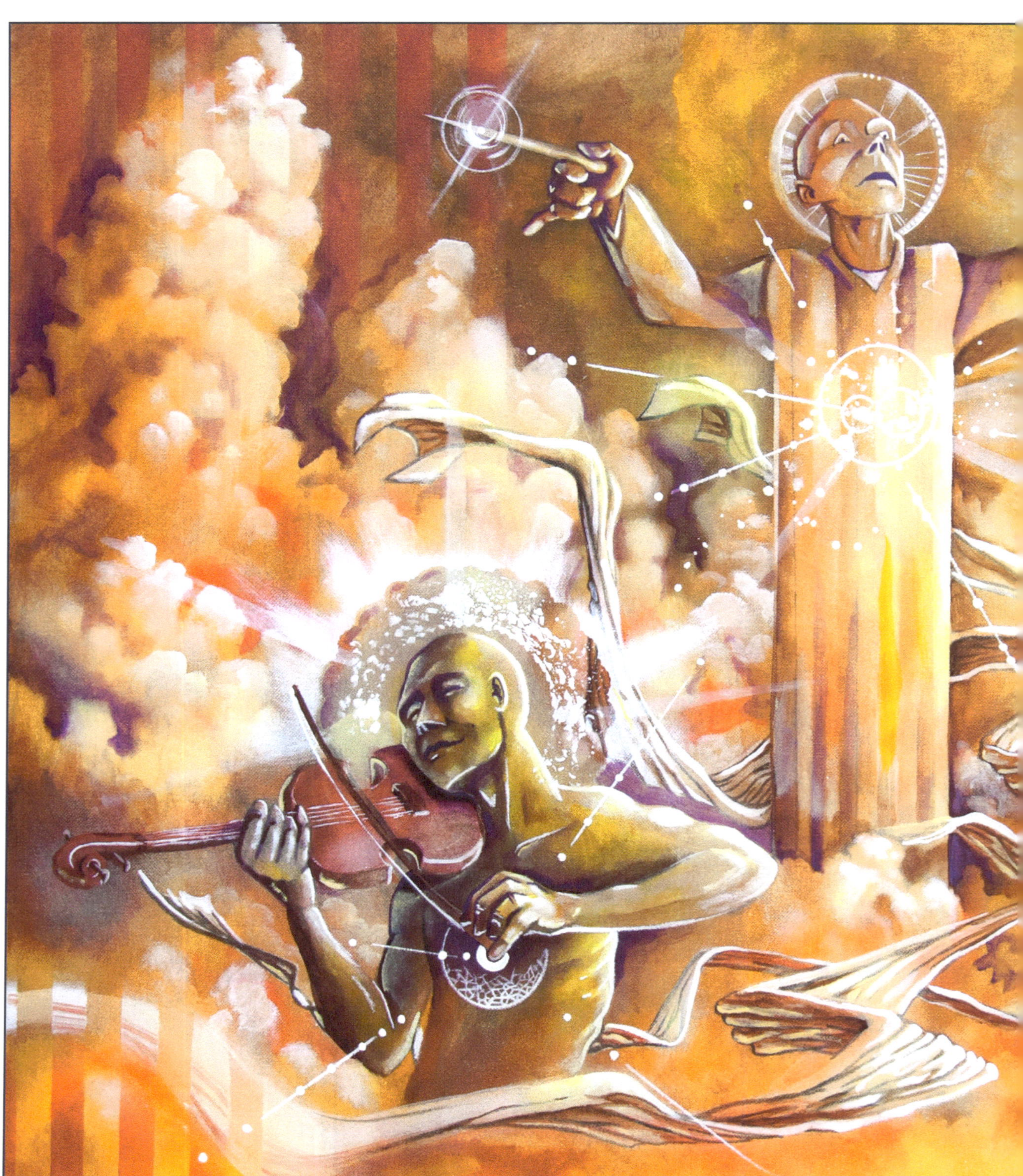

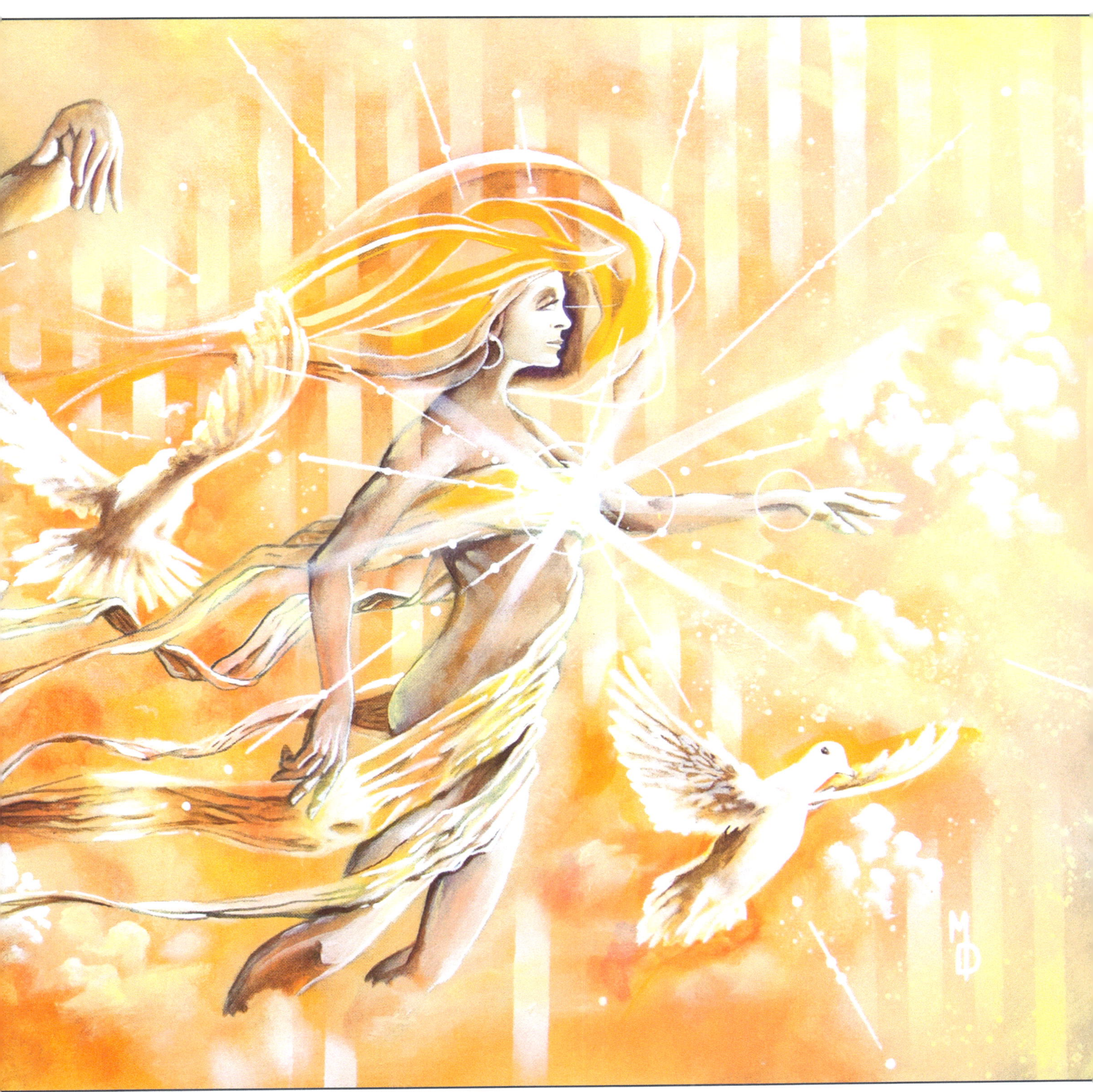

Serenading the Crossover, 2014
48"x24"
Acrylic & Mixed Media on Canvas

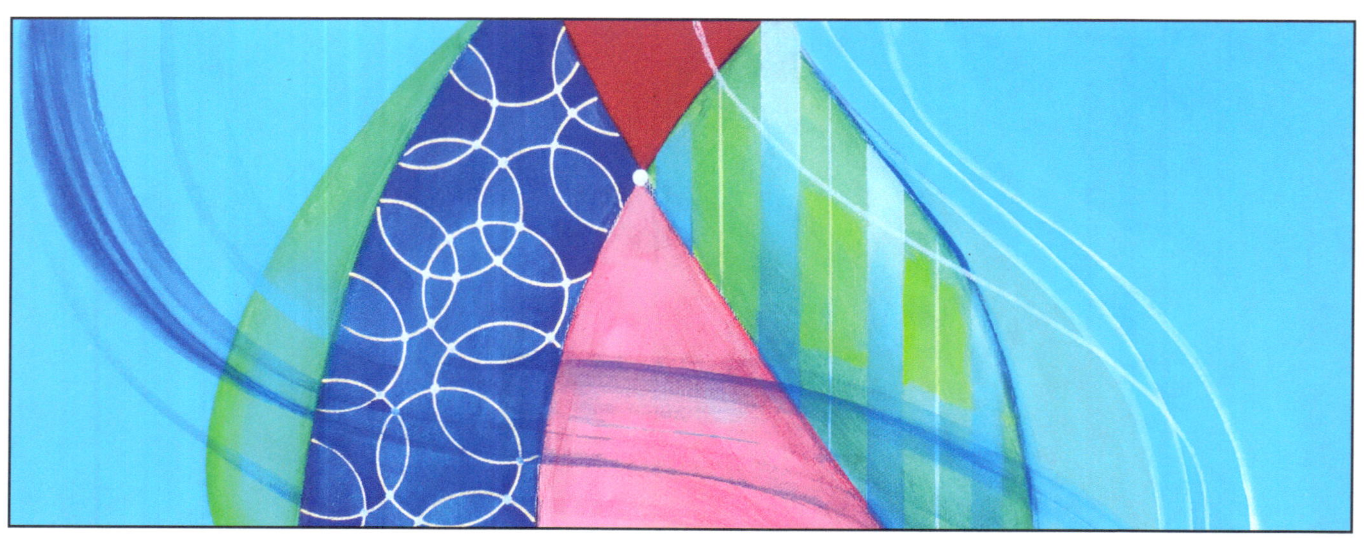

Miles continues to expand the Totem Series by exploring the principles in more abstract-leaning directions, playing with patterns and colors instead of a specific narrative.

Midnight Swirl, 2024
24"x48"
Acrylic & Mixed Media on Canvas
Blacklight Enhanced

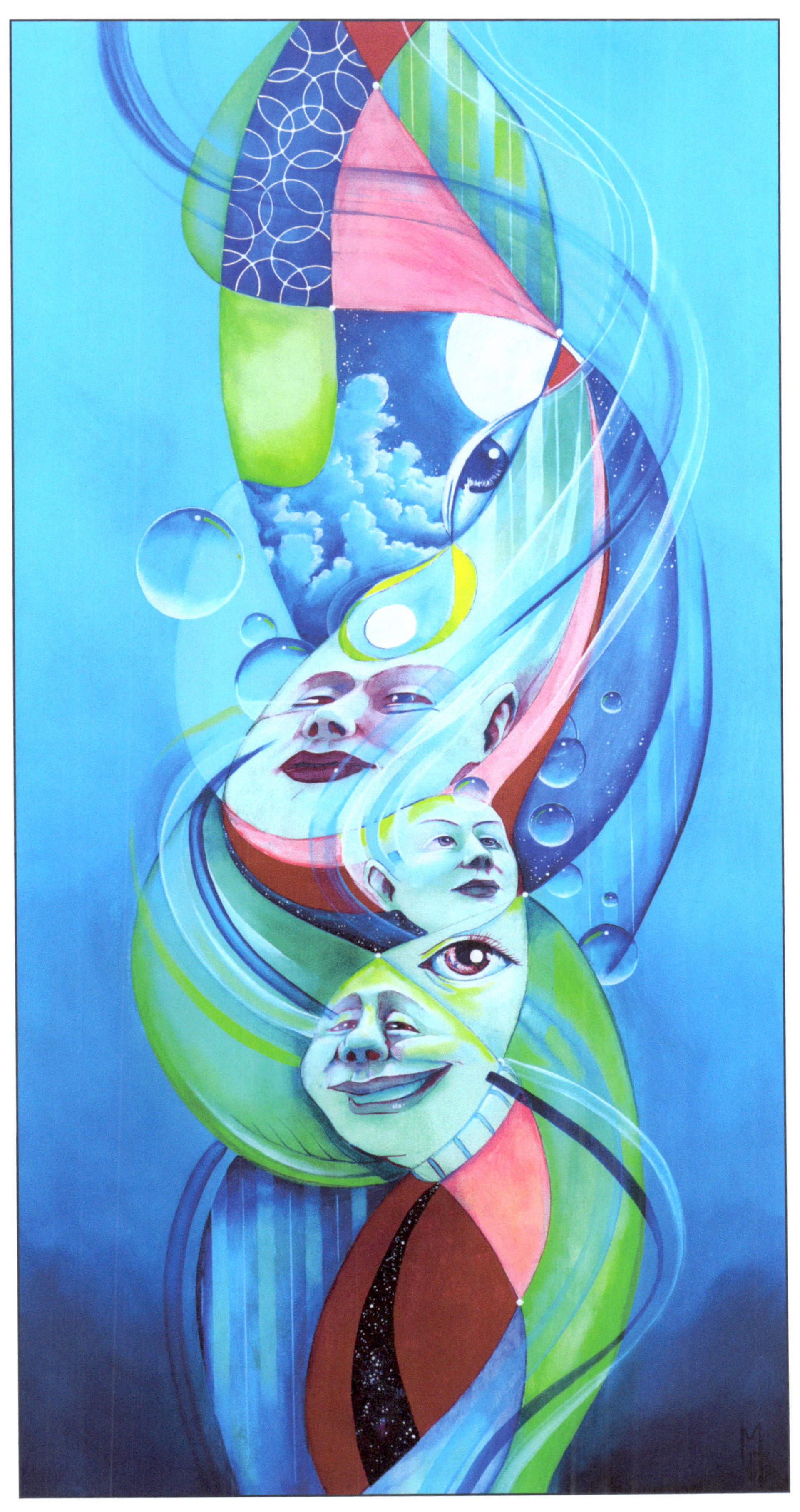

Infinity Painting

With no true beginning or end, *March of Life* is an infinity painting, meticulously designed to be repetitive. This diptych can be displayed left to right or right to left.

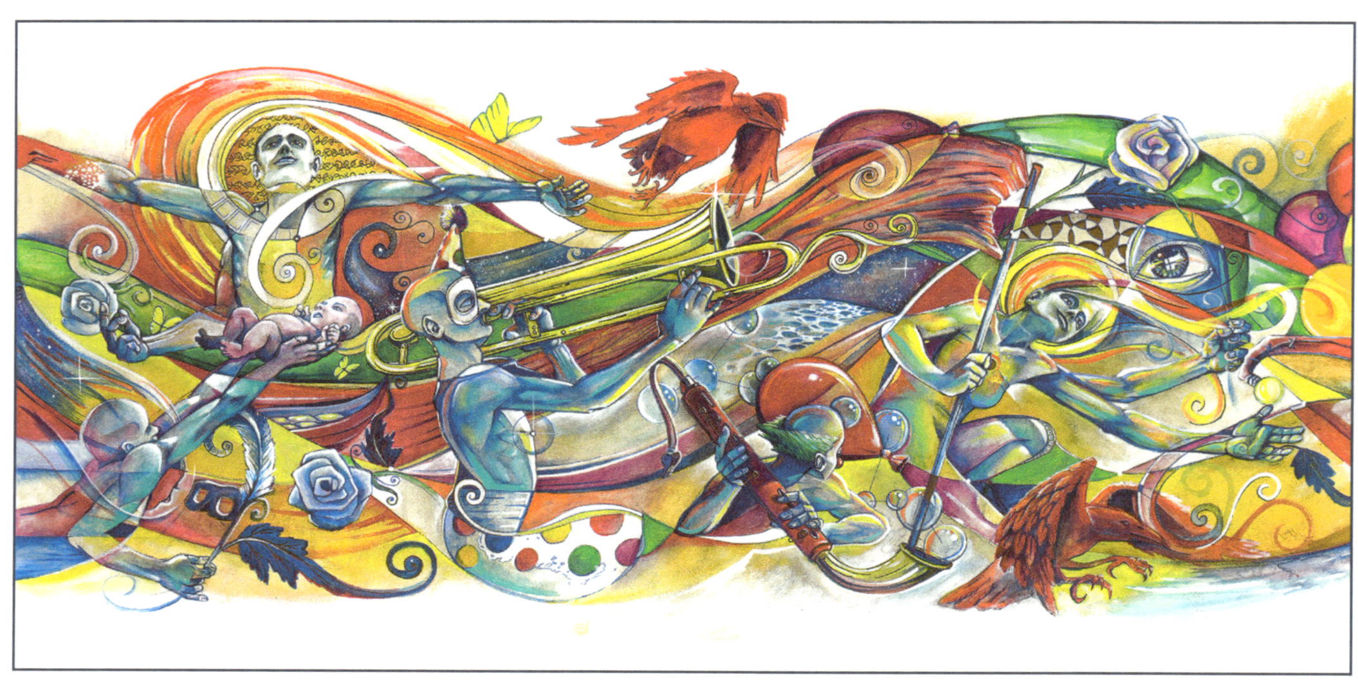

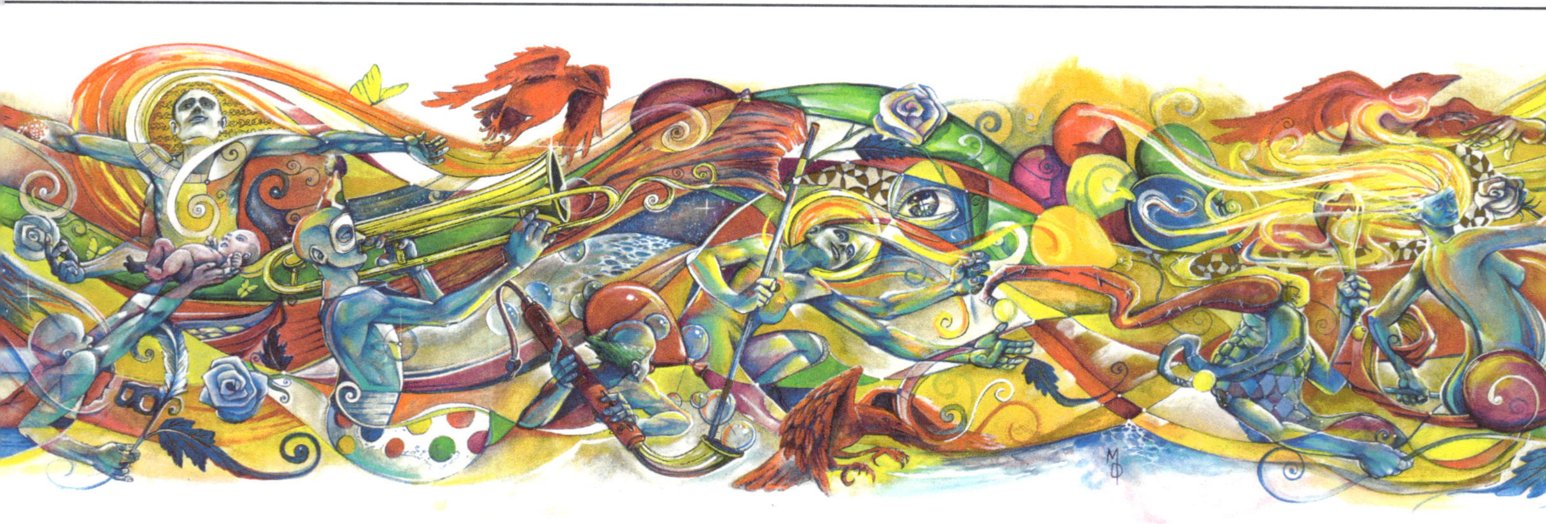

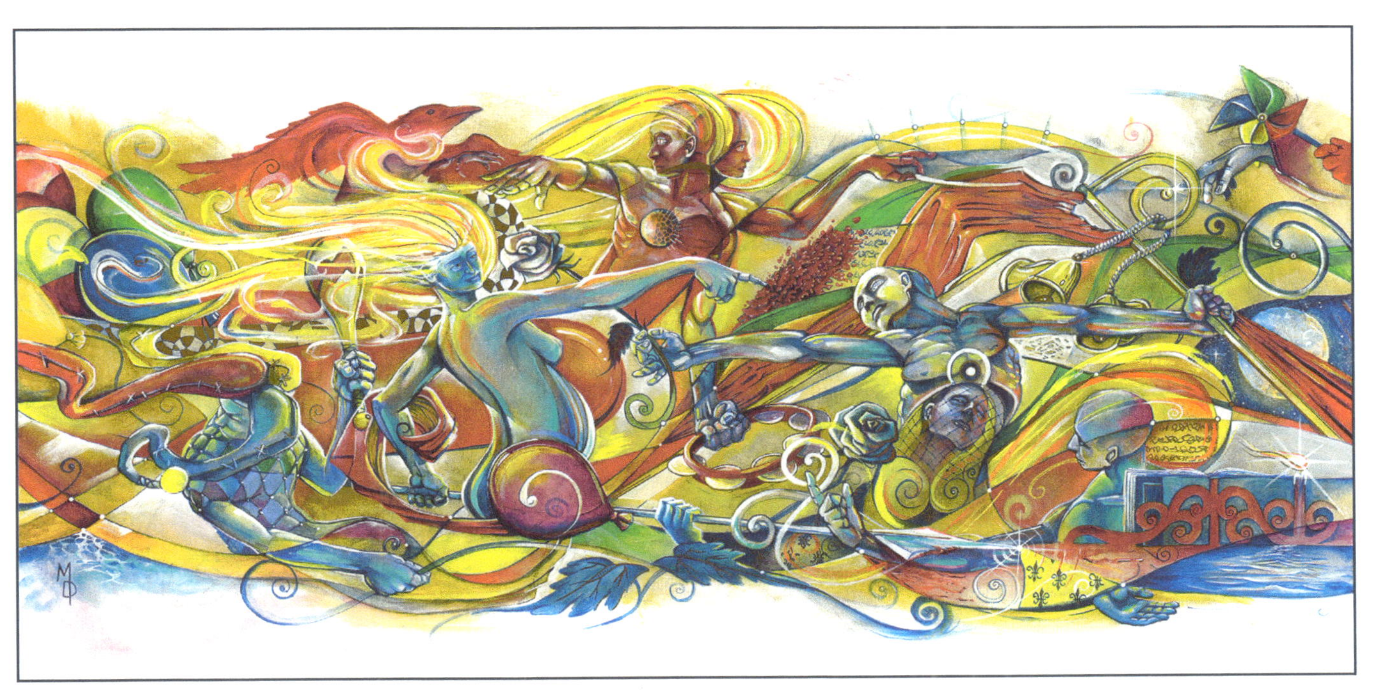

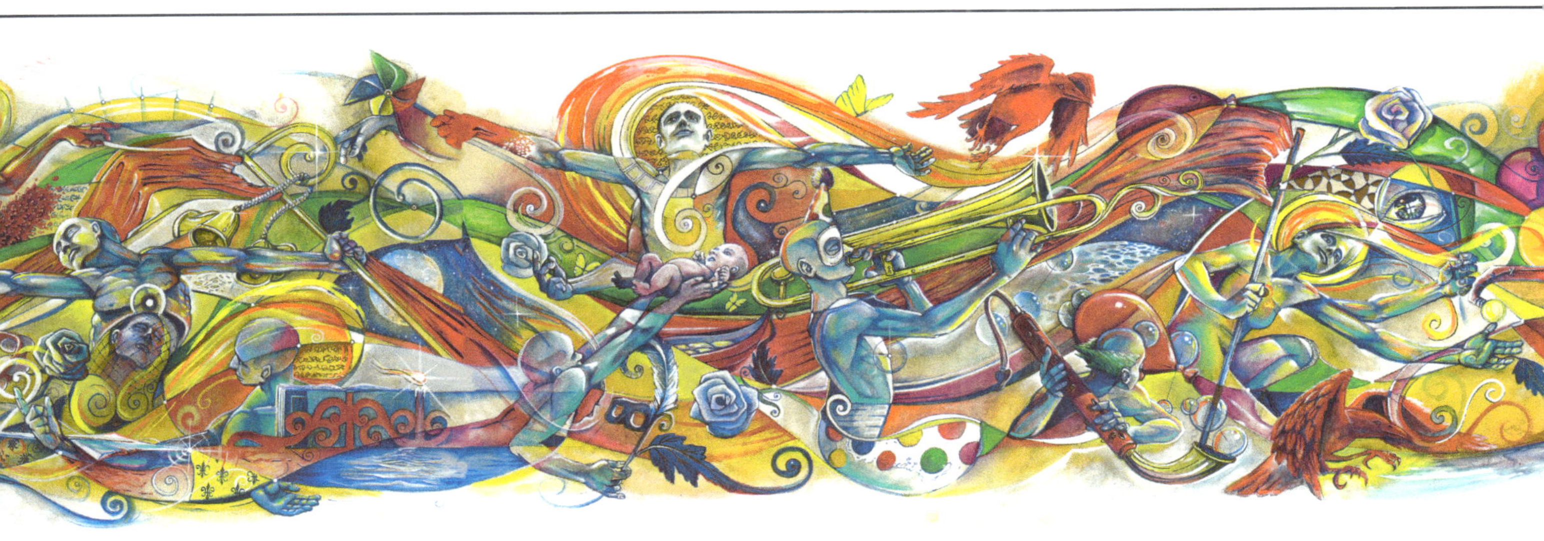

March of Life I & II, 2020
Diptych 96"x24"
Acrylic & Mixed Media on Canvas
Blacklight Enhanced

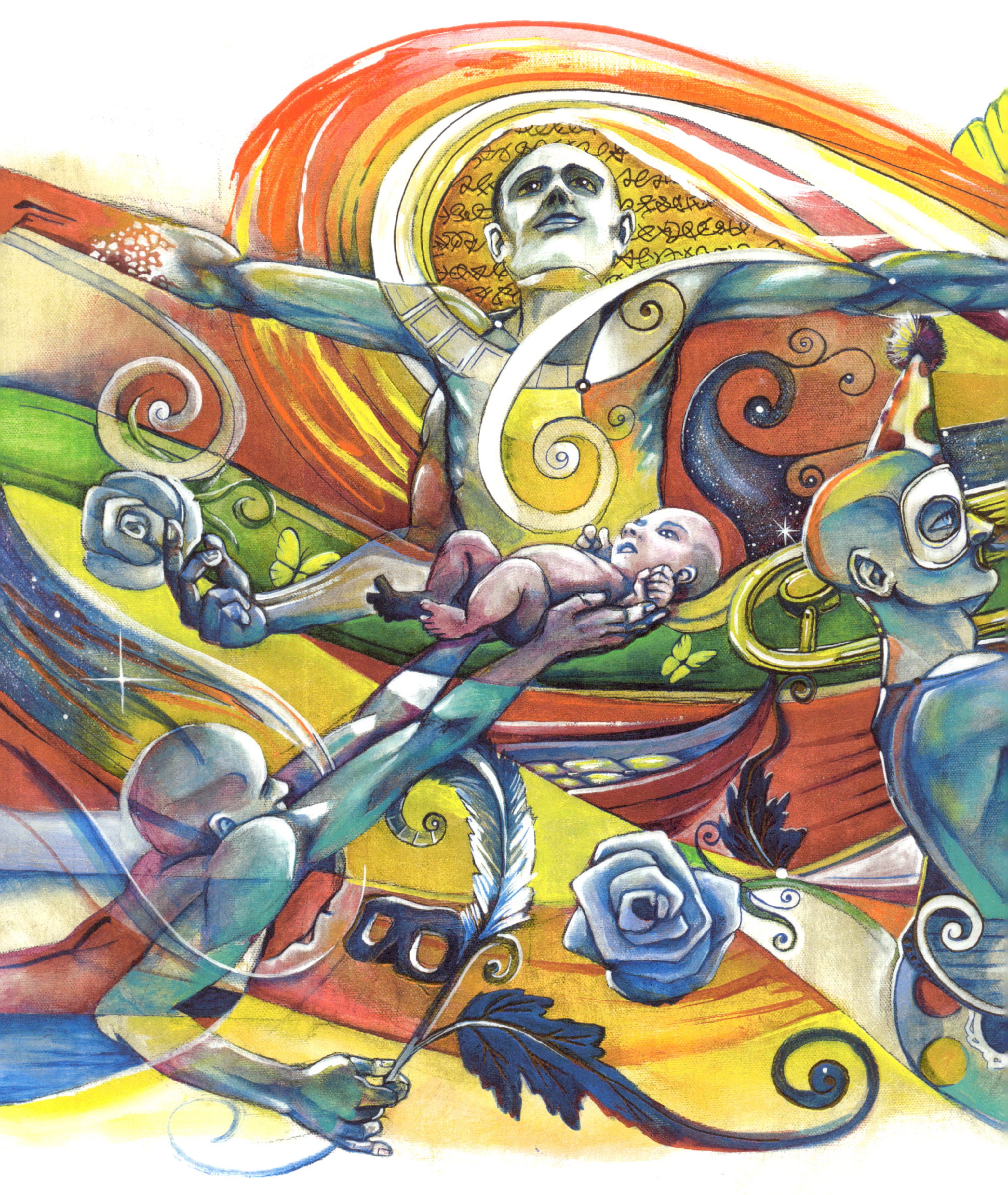

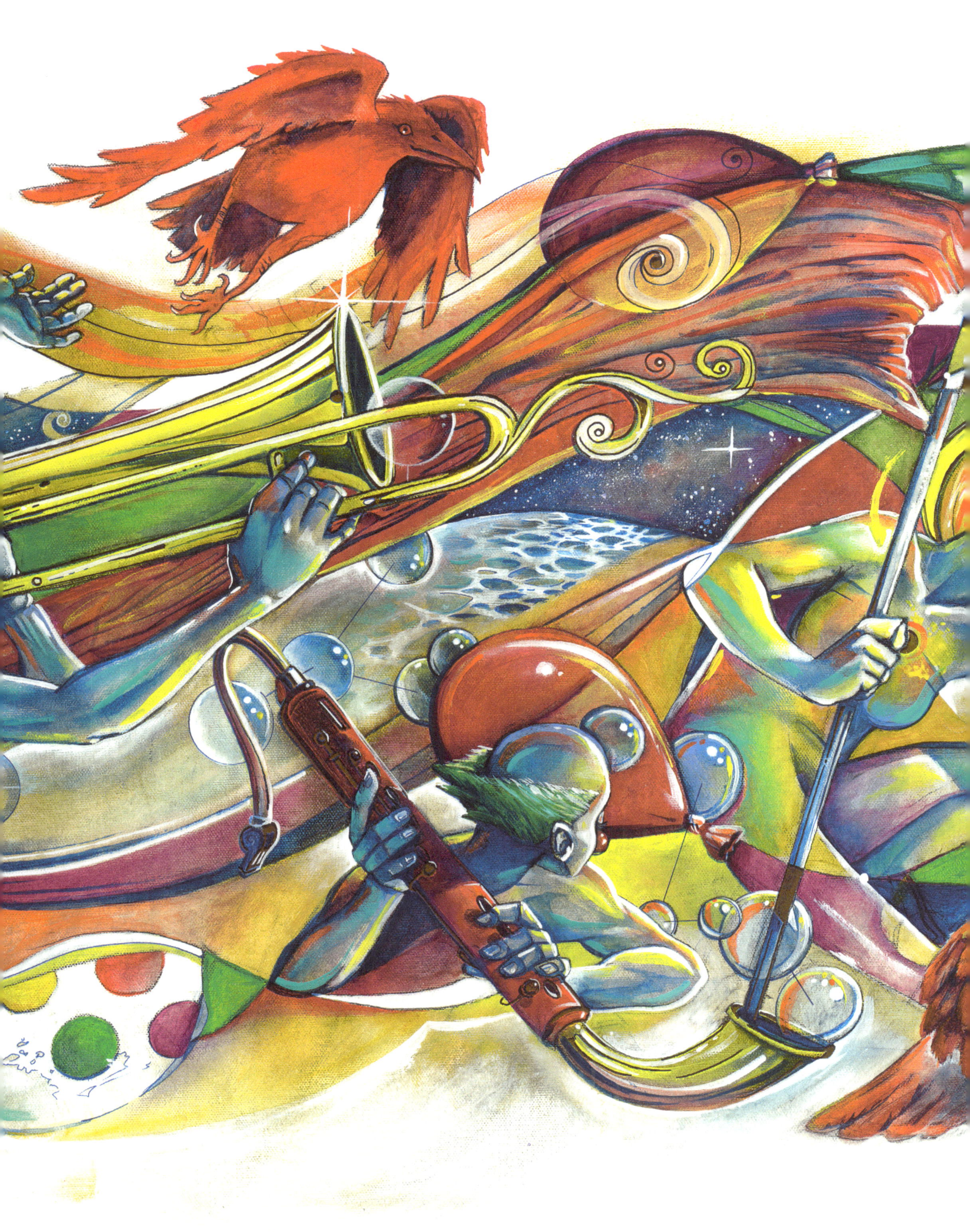

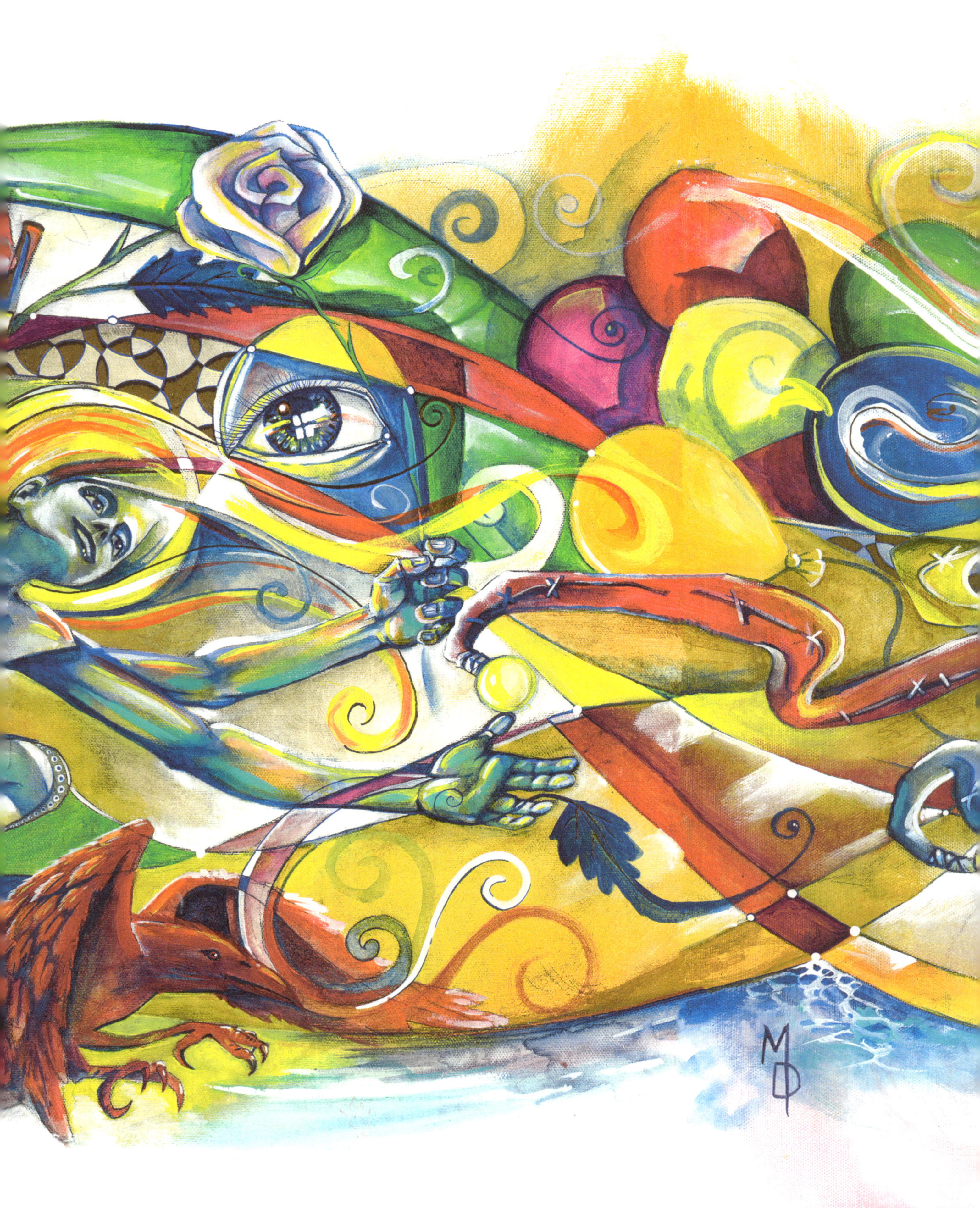

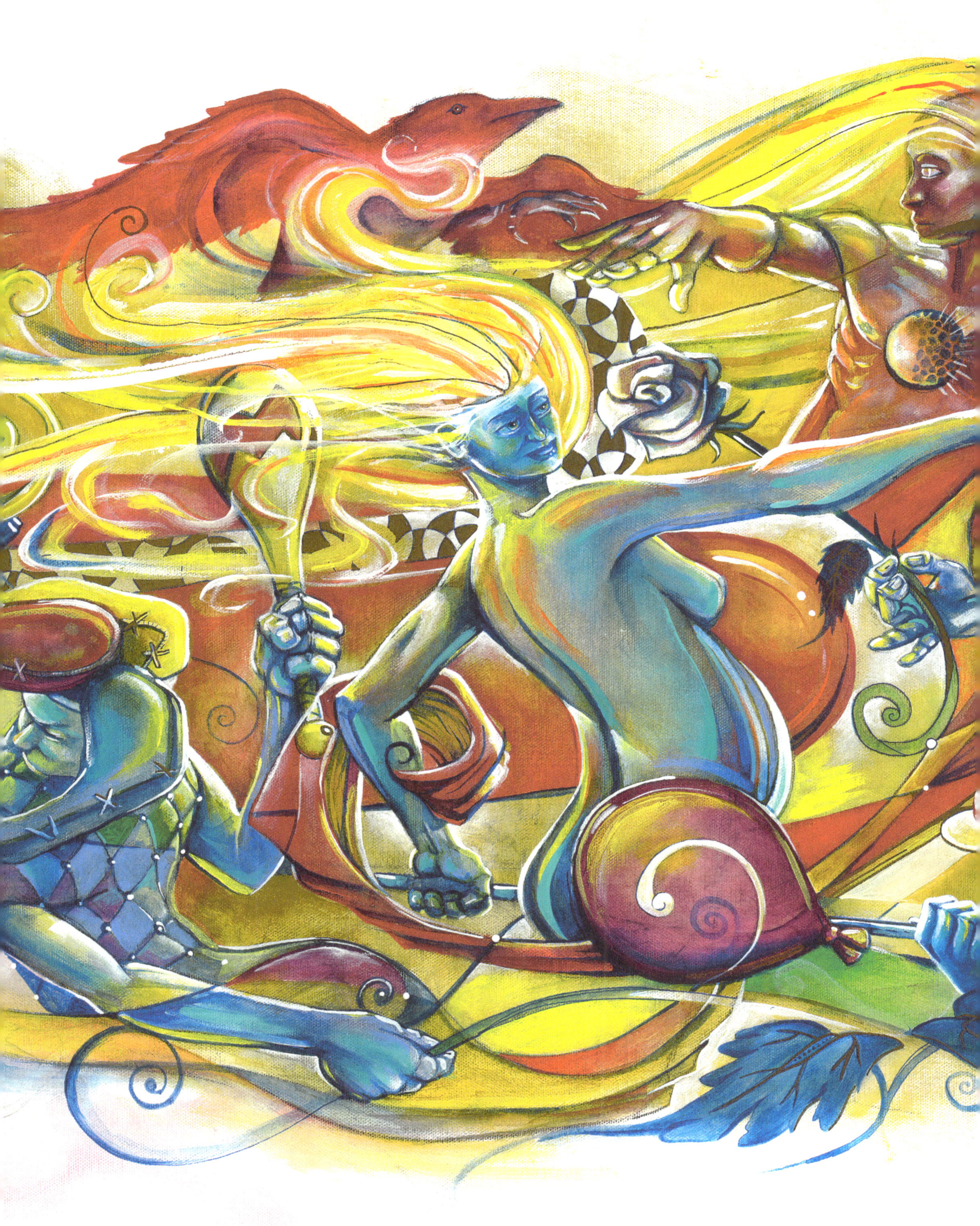

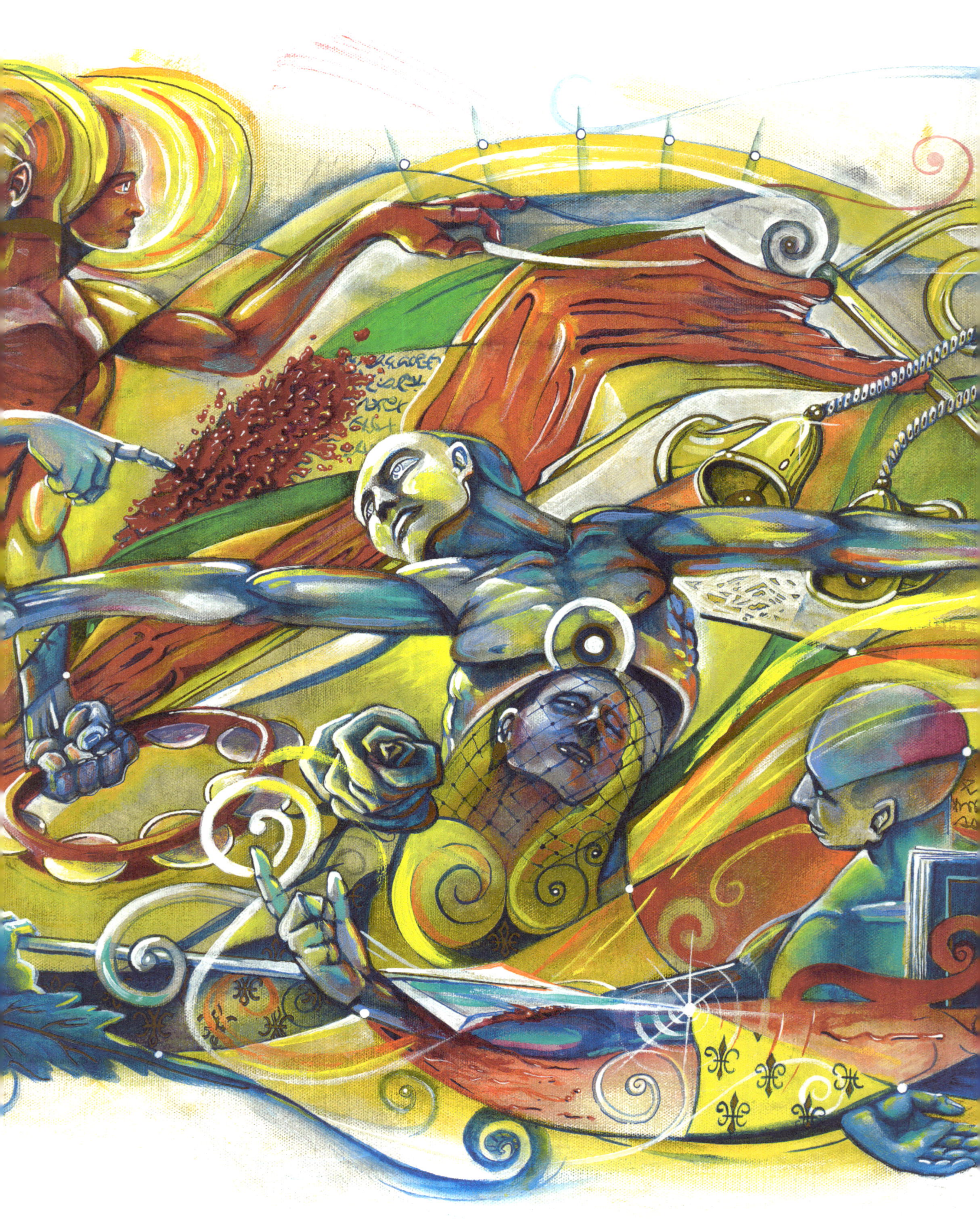

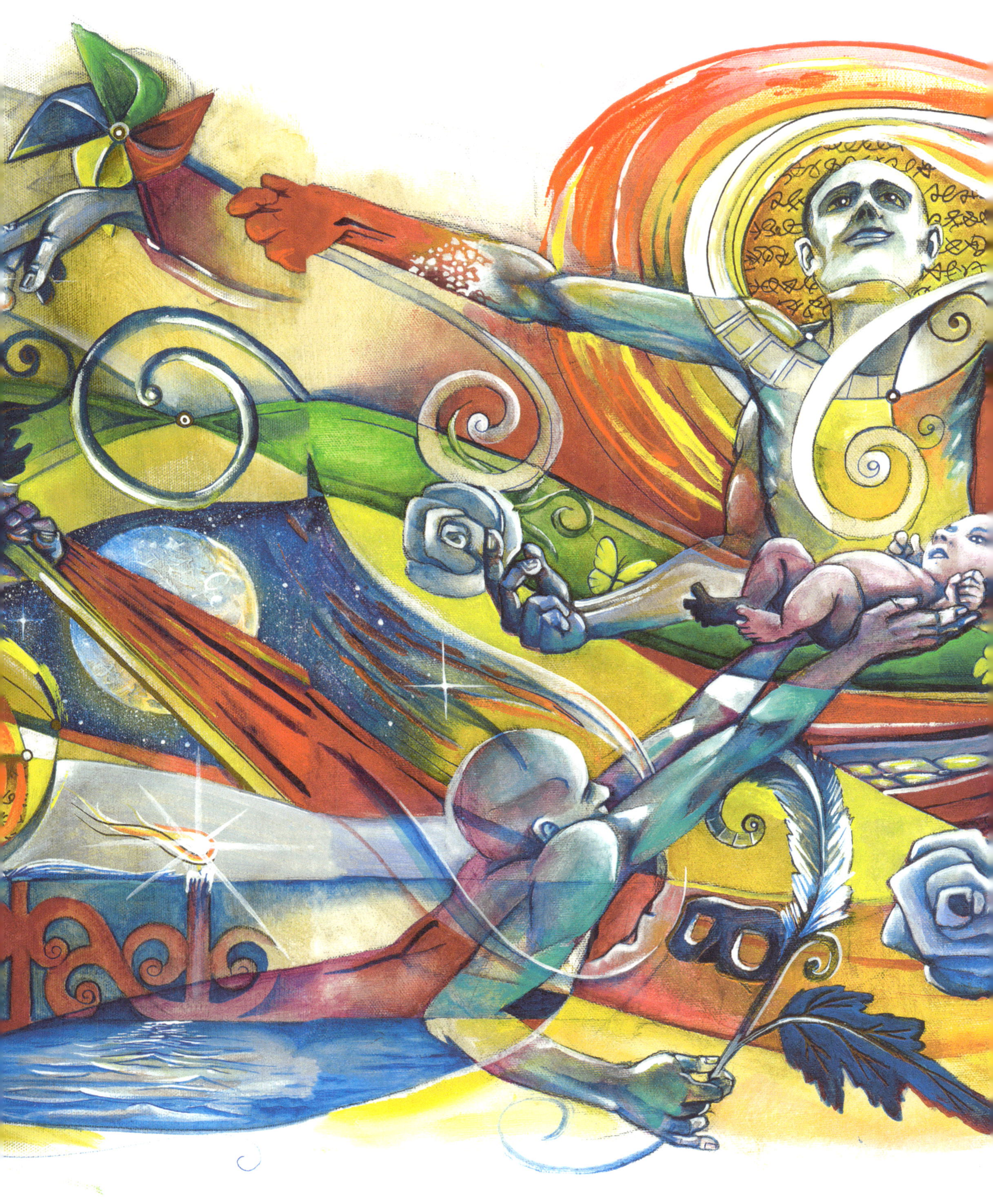

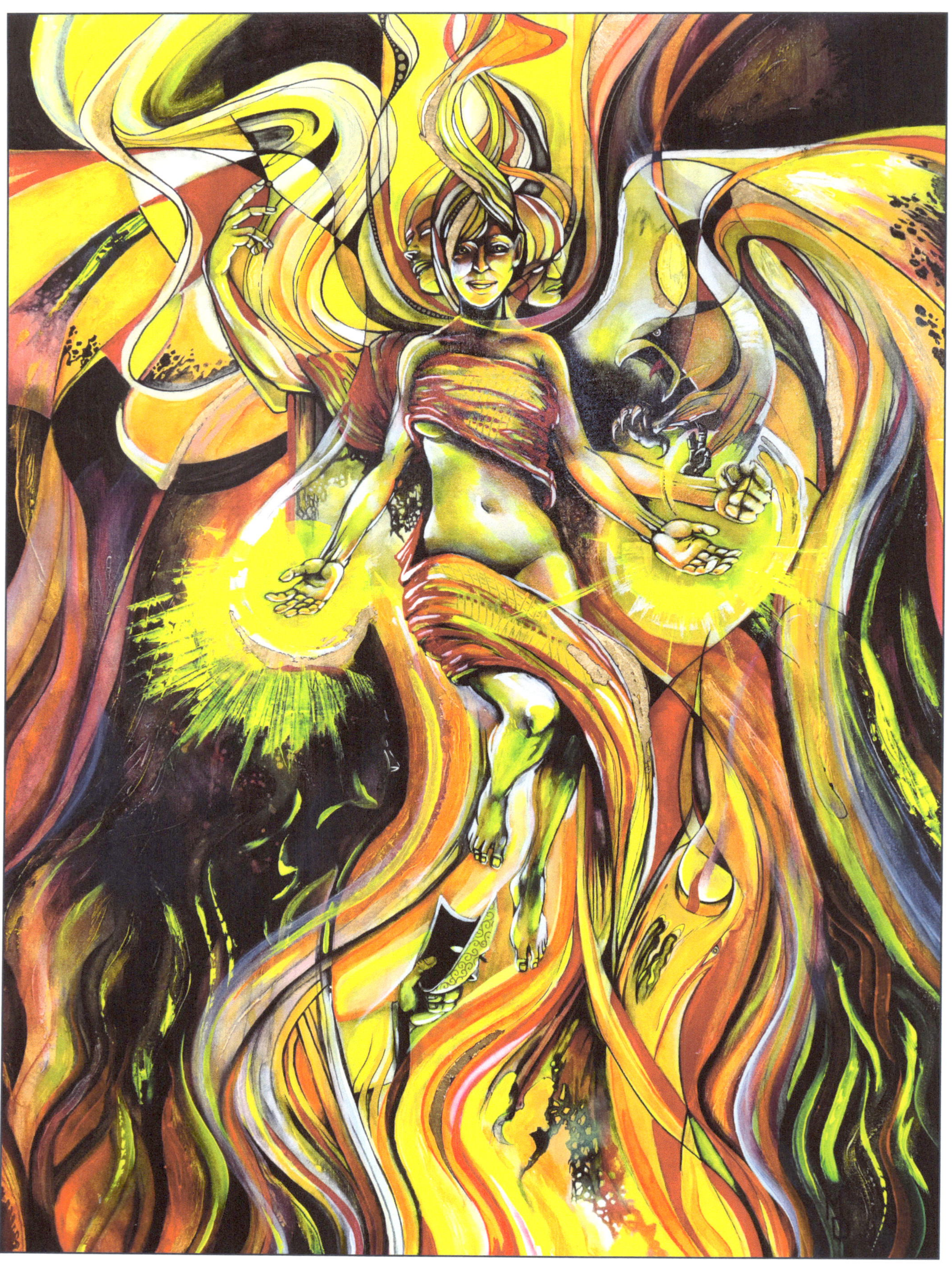

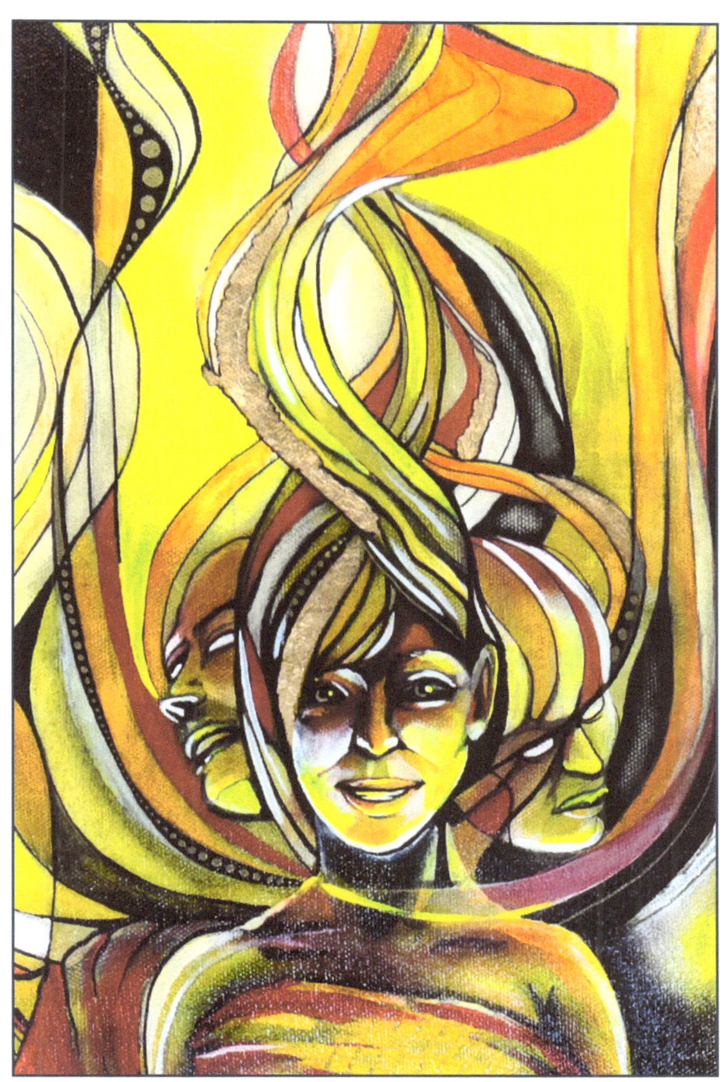

Phoenix Rising, 2023
30"x40"
Acrylic & Mixed Media on Canvas

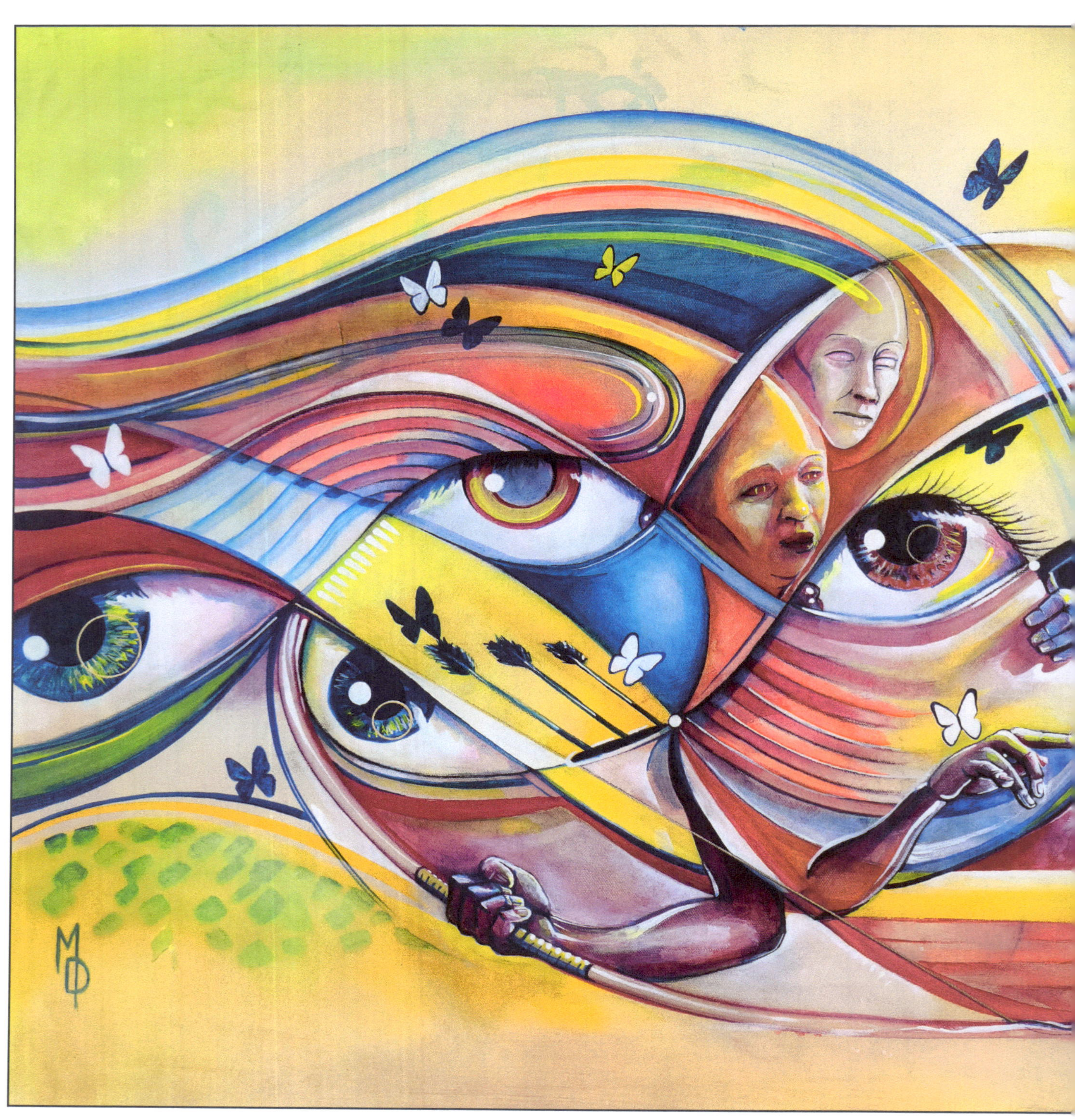

Fluttering Fates, 2024
48"x24"
Acrylic & Mixed Media on Canvas
Blacklight Enhanced

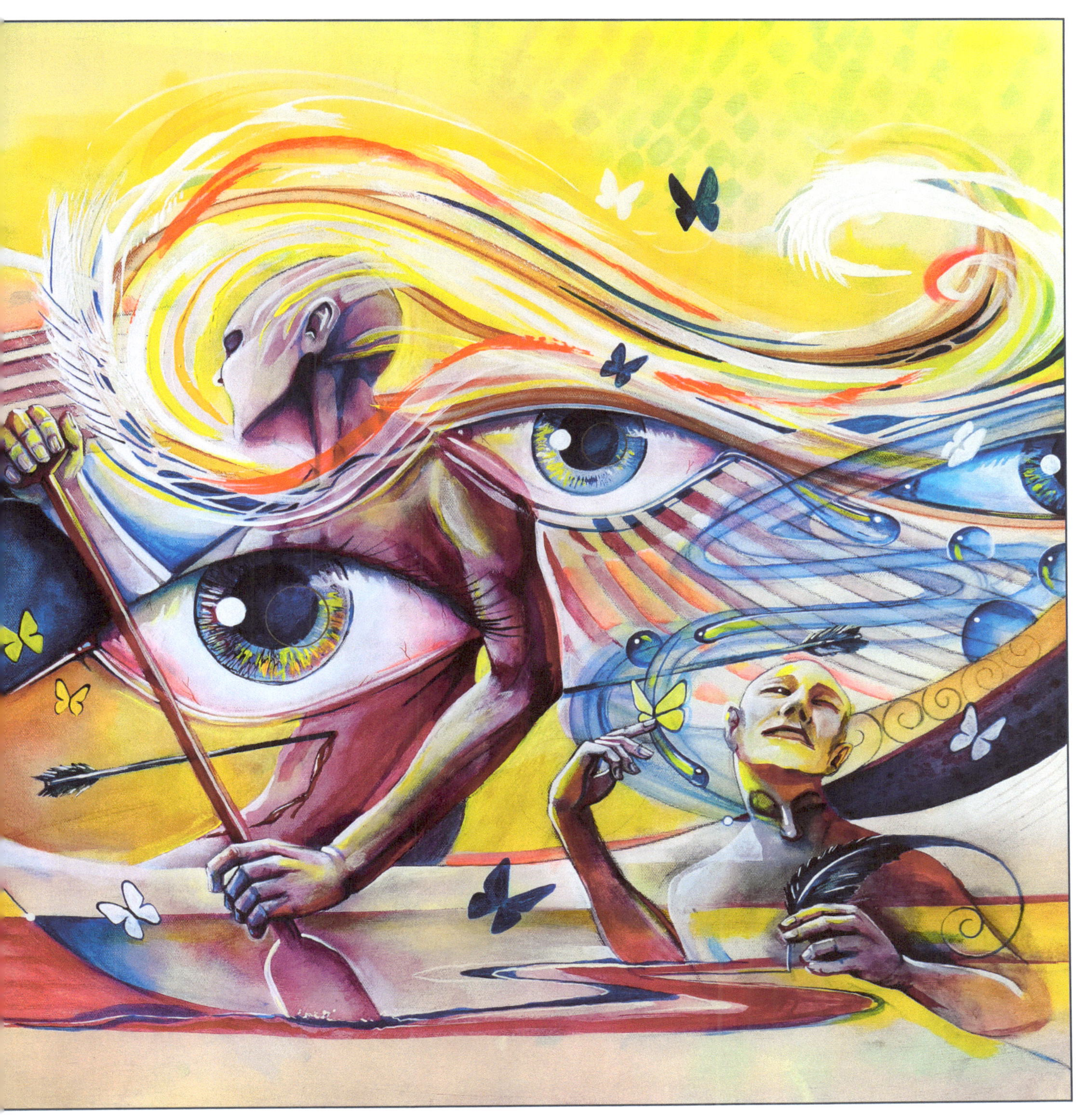

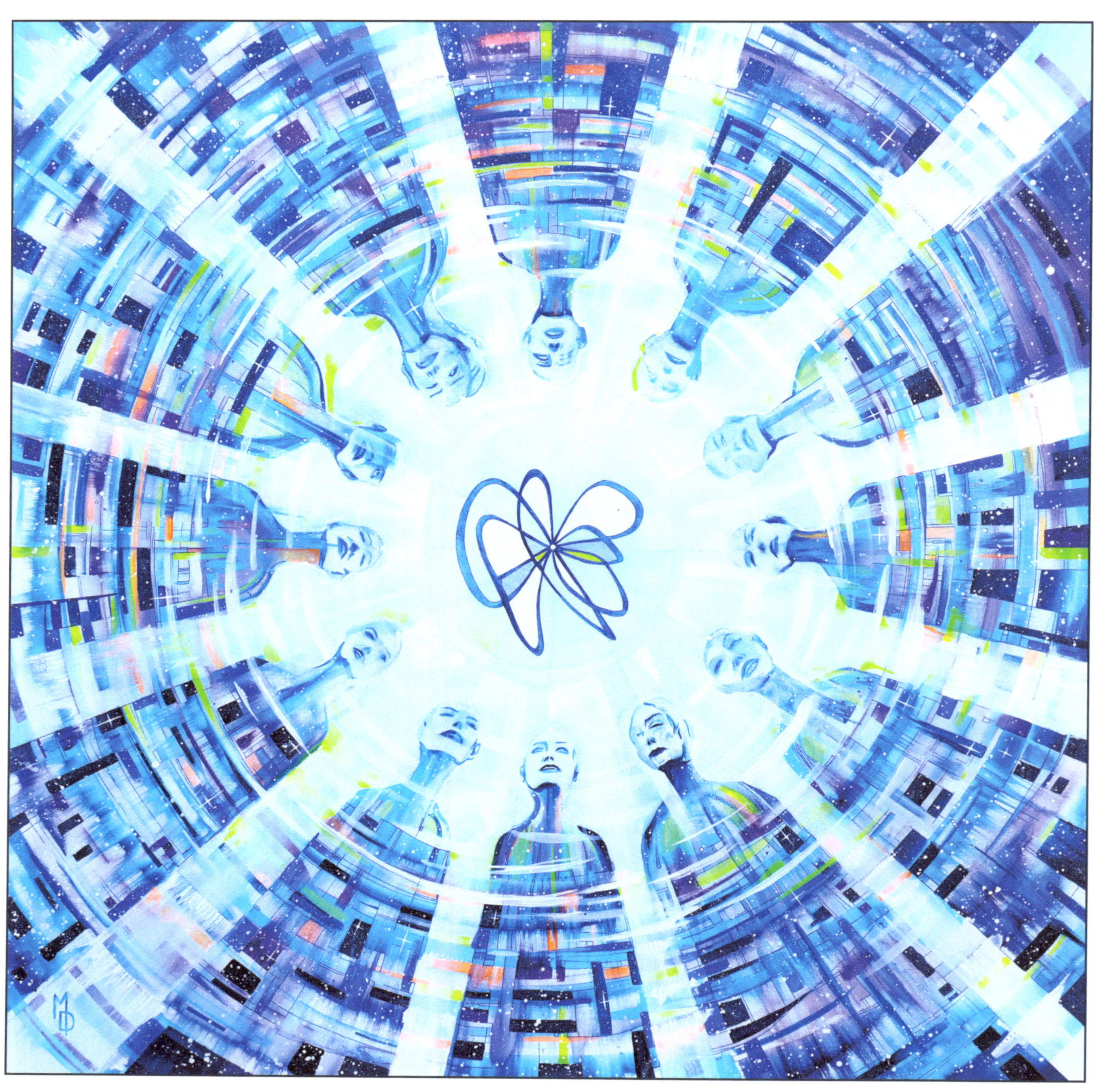

Collective Unconscious, 2022
48"x48"
Acrylic & Mixed Media on Canvas
Blacklight Enhanced

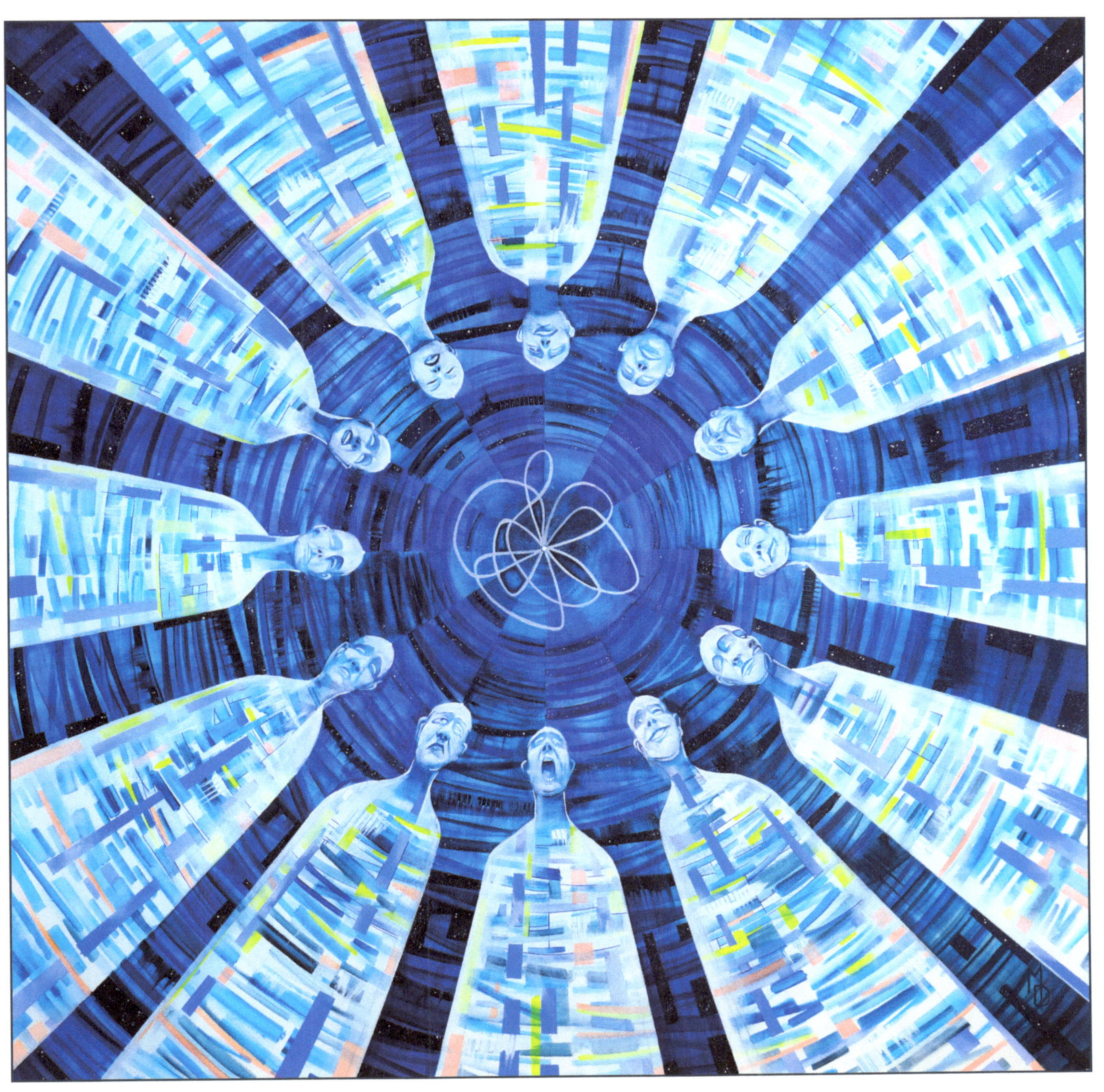

Collective Conscious, 2023
48"x48"
Acrylic & Mixed Media on Canvas
Blacklight Enhanced

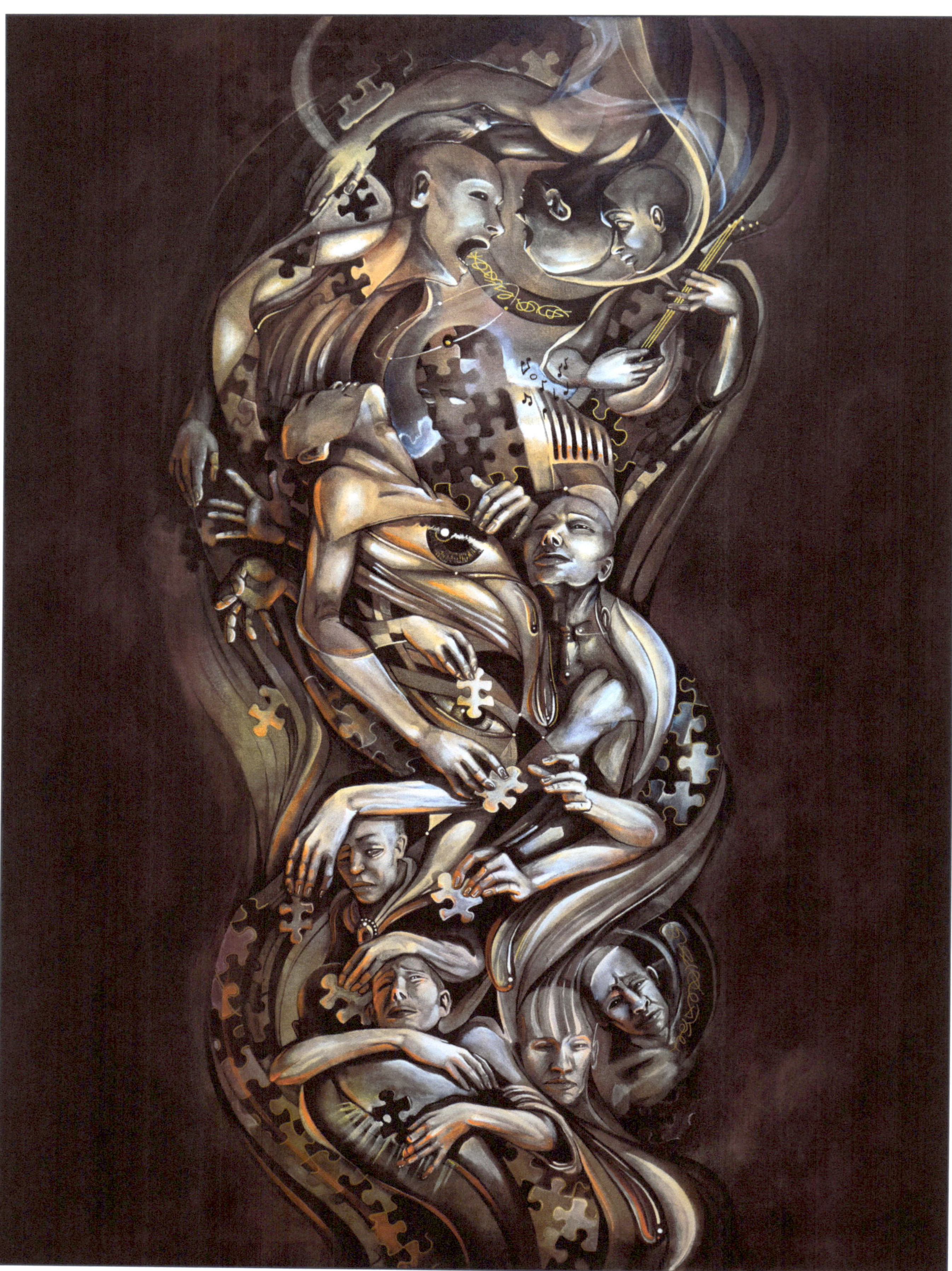

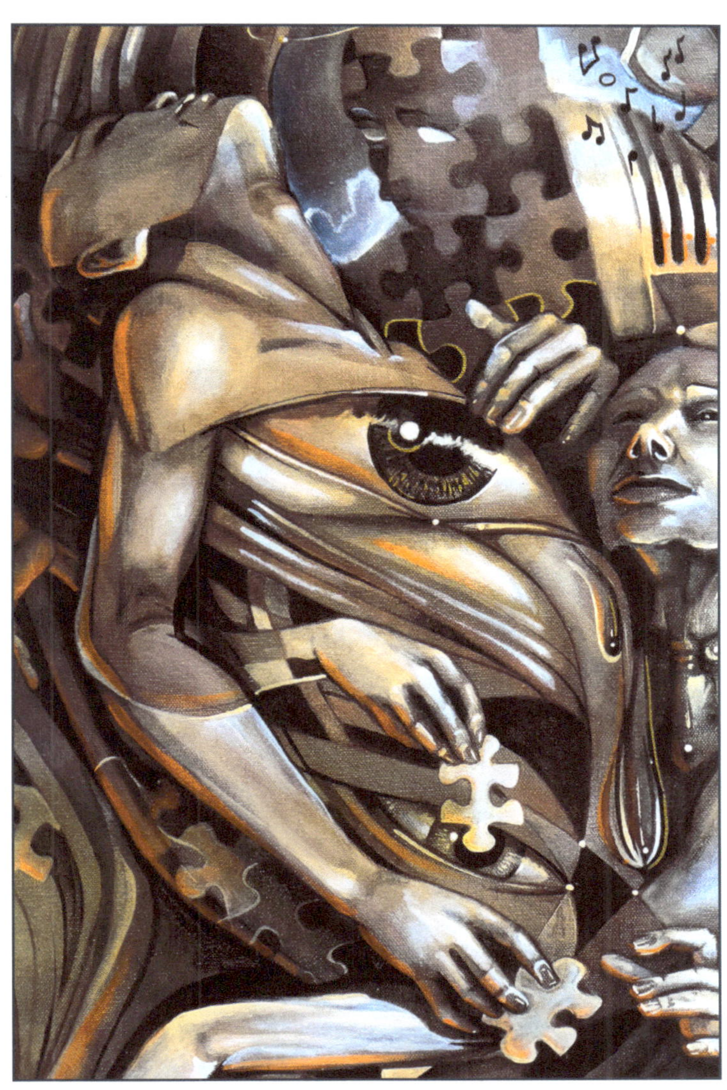

Bittersweet Nostalgia, 2024
36"x48"
Acrylic & Mixed Media on Canvas
Blacklight Enhanced

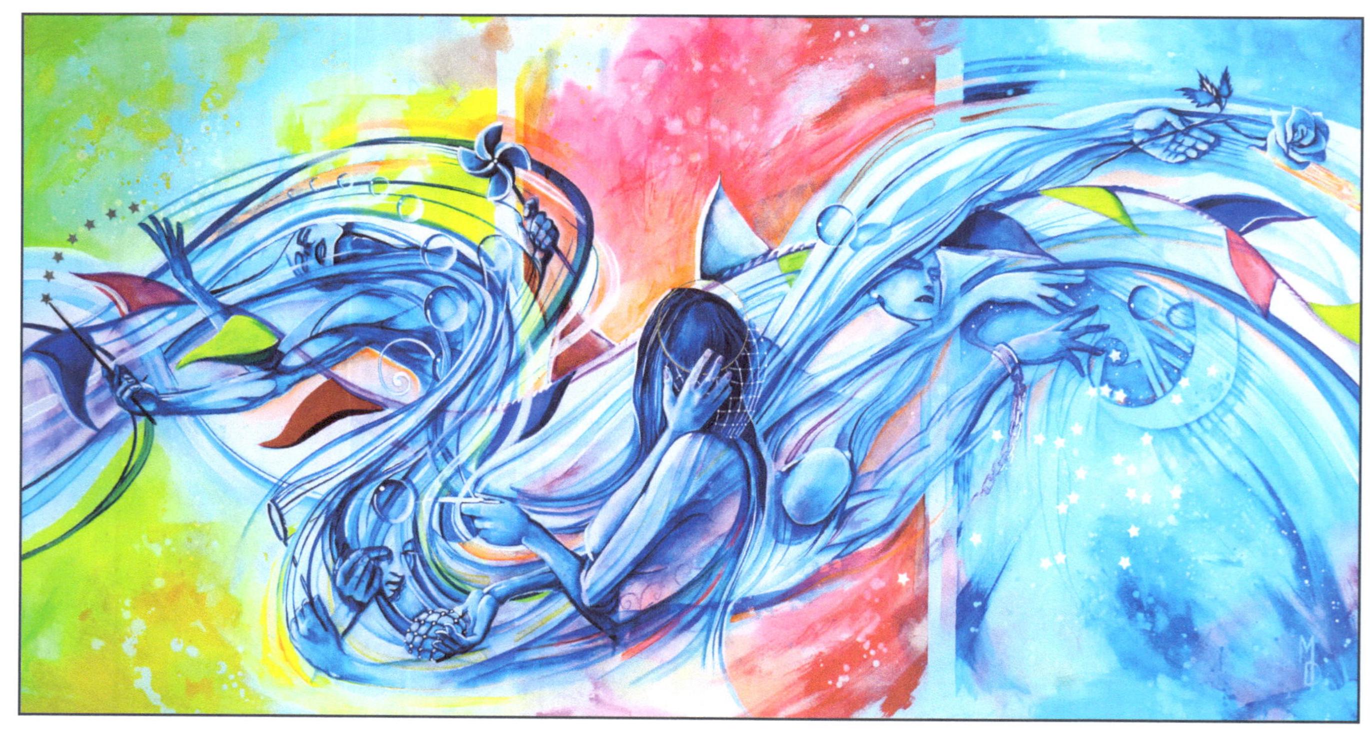

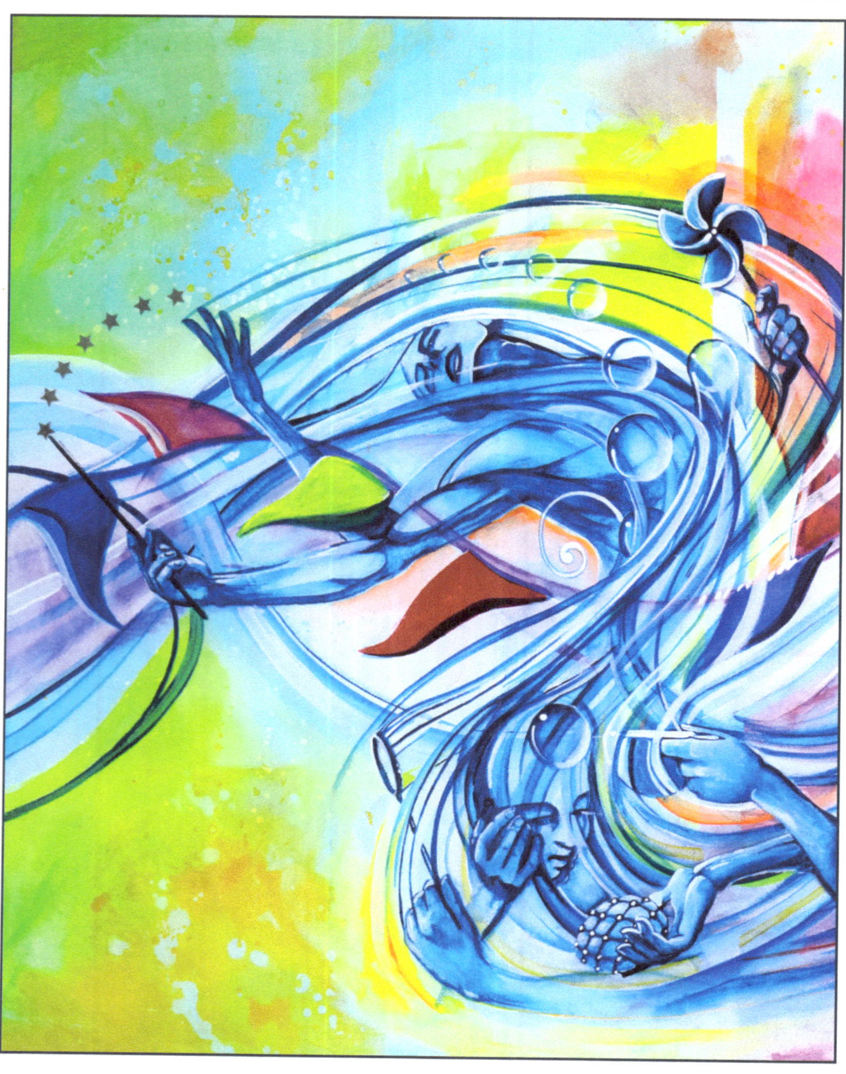

Fleeting Nature of Joy, 2023
48"x24"
Acrylic & Mixed Media on Canvas
Blacklight Enhanced

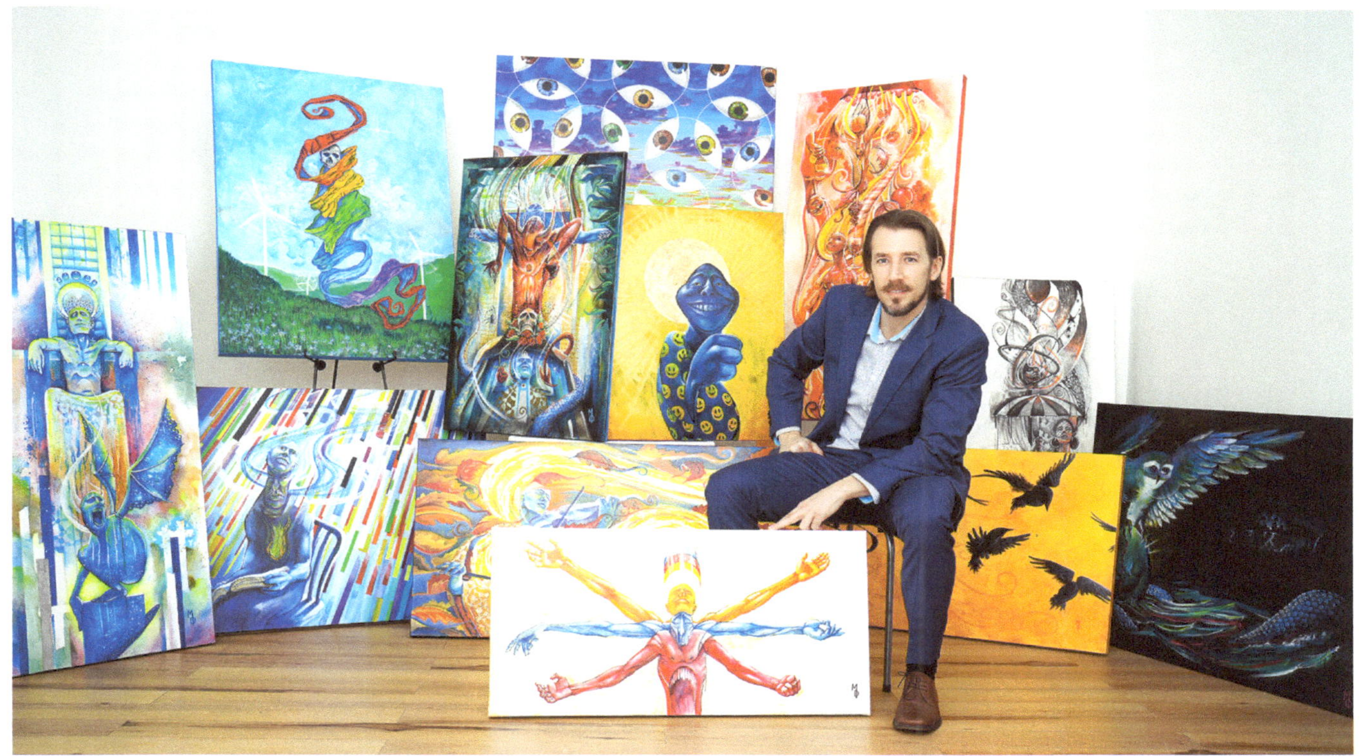

Miles Davis

Through painting, Miles explores the crossroads of modern spirituality and science and seeks to examine those complexities in an honest way. Inspired by the evolving relationship between personal and cultural identity, he uses crisp illustrative aesthetics and dramatic symbolism to engage the viewer. Striving for a unique accessibility, Miles endeavors to bypass perceived elitist tendencies and create work that speaks to everyone despite their art education.

Since 2003, Miles has been building his art practice through personal work, commissions, and public art. He has been included in grant projects from the National Endowment for the Arts and has received numerous awards for his paintings. Miles exhibits both nationally and internationally and made his debut solo museum exhibition in 2022 with "Vibrant Shadows" at the Marietta Cobb Museum of Art. For more information on Miles and his work, explore the other books in the Studio Collections series and visit massiveburn.com.

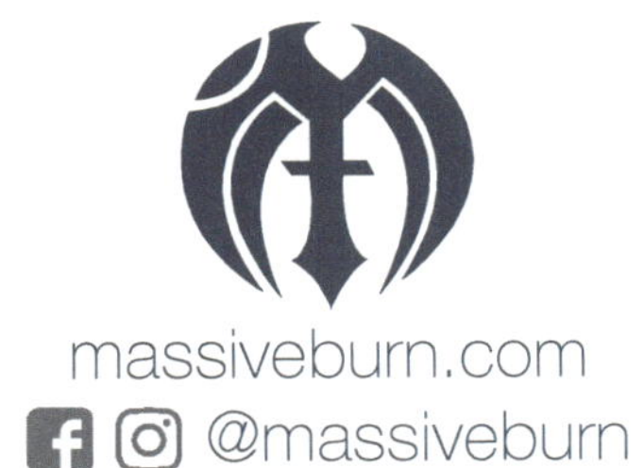

massiveburn.com

@massiveburn

www.ingramcontent.com/pod-product-compliance
Lightning Source LLC
LaVergne TN
LVHW070153110826
845147LV00002B/388
* 9 7 9 8 9 9 1 8 8 1 6 0 9 *